An Inexplicable Story

AN INEXPLICABLE STORY

or

THE NARRATIVE OF QUESTUS FIRMUS SICULUS

Josef Skvorecky

Translated from the Czech by Káča Poláčková Henley

KEY PORTER BOOKS

National Library of Canada Cataloguing in Publication Data

Skvorecky, Josef, 1924–
    An Inexplicable Story

ISBN 1-55263-368-3

I. Title.

PS8537.K86N37 2001   C813'.54   C2001-900605-5
PR9199.3.S58N37 2001

THE CANADA COUNCIL | LE CONSEIL DES ARTS
FOR THE ARTS | DU CANADA
SINCE 1957 | DEPUIS 1957

ONTARIO ARTS COUNCIL
CONSEIL DES ARTS DE L'ONTARIO

The publisher gratefully acknowledges the support of the Canada Council for the Arts and the Ontario Arts Council for its publishing program.

We acknowledge the financial support of the Government of Canada through the Book Publishing Industry Development Program (BPIDP) for our publishing activities.

Key Porter Books Limited
70 The Esplanade
Toronto, Ontario
Canada M5E 1R2
www.keyporter.com

Cover design: Peter Maher
Electronic formatting: Heidy Lawrance Associates

Printed and bound in Canada

02 03 04 05 06 07 6 5 4 3 2 1

PREFACE
TO THE FIRST
(DOLPHIN LIBRARY)
EDITION

The history of the discovery of the so-called Questus manuscript has been amply described in both the academic and the popular press. It was found in Honduras by a group of Miskatonic University students of Mayan archaeology, on a dig overseen by Professor Howard Phillips Langhorn, in the structure designated Rosalie at the acropolis at Copán. A cracked pottery urn inscribed with the words *Narratio Questi* (apparently gilded originally) was discovered in the wall of a royal tomb containing the physical remains of a man who may very well have been K'inich Yax K'uk'Mo', who lived in the early fourth century A.D. and founded a dynasty that over several centuries shaped Copán. The manuscript consists of seven narrow scrolls, and appears—from the internal evidence of the partially preserved text—to have been written in an undetermined pre-Mayan town on the Atlantic coast. How it found its way to the landlocked kingdom of Copán is unclear. It is surmised that it was simply brought there, perhaps revered as a relic of the visit from the "white gods" mentioned in some of the legends of Central American peoples.

The manuscript, written in black ink on a kind of Roman paper made from Egyptian papyrus known as *charta fanniana* (from its manufacturer, Fannius), has been subjected to every available physical test, and its language to detailed scholarly scrutiny, since there was understandably a suspicion that it might be a hoax. After repeated tests and analyses, however, the experts concurred: it is in fact an authentic Roman manuscript dating from the first century A.D., written in the Latin used by intellectuals in the time of Augustus.

Although the scrolls themselves appeared to be genuine, a deeper mystery remained: how had a Latin text from the time of the early Empire come to be in the Western hemisphere? It was hoped that an examination and interpretation of the text itself would provide an answer—a singularly challenging task in view of the severely deteriorated condition of the scrolls. The resulting conclusions, however, belie our current assumptions about the Roman Empire at the turn of the millennium and alter our view of the distances travelled by Roman seafarers, whose voyages were thought to have been limited to the Mediterranean, the Adriatic and Aegean seas, the Atlantic coast of today's France, both sides of what we know as the English Channel, and the Black Sea along the coast of today's Romania.

What follows is an English version of the Latin texts, based on the translation by Professor H. P.

Langhorn of Miskatonic University, which I have tried to adapt stylistically to the needs of the lay reader, all the while striving to omit nothing, add nothing, and distort nothing that would contradict scholarly interpretations. For the quotations from the poetry of Ovid, I have used the modern translations of Peter Green, in the Penguin editions of the poems.

Commentaries in italic type have been inserted to connect the textual fragments where hypothetical conclusions offered themselves, based on Professor Langhorn's scholarly theories. I have annotated the text only where I feel that context is essential to a grasp of the subject matter. As for names and events which do not arise elsewhere in literature from or about Rome and which play no significant role in the story, I only comment on these when an explanation is necessary for specific reasons.

The fragments are numbered and arranged chrono-logically, in so far as it is possible—tentatively—to deduce a chronology from the recovered text. Words that could be extrapolated contextually are in paren-theses. The text also includes Professor Langhorn's measurements of text that was indecipherable as a result of dampness and other environmental factors inside the cracked urn.

Patrick Oliver Enfield

NARRATIO QUESTI

SCROLL I

The manuscript is written in the Roman manner, in columns about five centimetres wide, each containing twenty-two to twenty-five lines of an average twenty letters each. Words in parentheses indicate that the word, incomplete or illegible in the Latin text, was deduced from the context by the translator. Text in square brackets is Professor Langhorn's estimate of the length of an illegible or missing section of the text, abbreviated as follows:

wd/s	=	Word/s
l/s	=	Line/s
col/s	=	Column/s

* * *

The initial six columns are badly damaged, with only truncated fragments remaining legible:

FRAGMENT

I

consulate [1 l] Firmus Siculus[1]

---

[1] We discover further on in the text that this man is Questus's father and that his given name is Gaius. In the Republic, a three-name system was used, and it prevailed into the Empire, until

2

(wings) of Icarus [2–3 wds] did not resemble wings at all but did in fact fly. It was a round stick topped perpendicularly with two thin flat pieces of [3–4 wds]. When twirled between one's (palms)

---

finally utter confusion resulted. The use of three names remained the rule, but as a result of adoption, the splitting of original families, the loss of the original significance of the surname, or the awarding of a special honour (*cognomen ex virtute*), the original name could expand to five or even more units; a citizen could end up bearing the pretentious appellation "Publius Cornelius Scipio Nasica Corculum," etc. This, of course, applied only to the Roman aristocracy, members of the order of knights (*equites* or *equester ordo*), and senators (*senatores*). The first of the three names, in this case Gaius, is the *praenomen* and designates the given individual. The second, the *nomen*—here, Firmus—designates the clan (*gens*), and the third—Siculus—is the *cognomen*, the family name. The son of Gaius, then, is Questus Firmus Siculus. His mother is Proculeia, from the Aemilius clan (hence "Aemilia," the feminine form of her father's name) Saepuli, which is the genitive (possessive) form of her father's *cognomen*. While there were other systems of names under the Empire, they are not relevant here, and I shall not go into them.

Still on the topic of names, it is interesting to note the *praenomen* of the narrator, Questus. Unlike our era, when a myriad of first names are in broad use, in the earliest times, the number of common *praenomina* was smaller than thirty. By the middle of the first century B.C., this list had shrunk to a mere eighteen. The name Questus is not among them. Perhaps it is a throwback to earlier times. In any case, it is another mystery in this tale of so many mysteries.

3

Alomeius, a shepherd on the isle of Ilva[2] [2–3 wds]
also carved likenesses of the (gods) [4–5 wds] brought
[2–3 wds] mother a statue of Venus carved in ebony,
and when he left, mother (told) her friend Letitia
Catullae that it's natural and (that he) certainly would
not give her Hercules. That made them both (laugh)

4

beautiful white teeth that father envied him. But [1
l] extremely remote. The middle names were
(different). He used to visit us often, but when I was
older, it seemed to me [1 l] as if she had not seen
him for a year. After that, I noticed

5

he enjoyed (bringing) me toys. So I had more than
plenty of [3 ls] three windmills made of tubes [3 ls]
windmills really spun (around). After giving birth, his
wife was crippled and the baby (died?)

6

and I enjoyed riding with mother [1 wd] the Aventine[3]
on a litter carried by six (bearers) and I always settled
down in (mother's) lap and watched the bearers'
backs in their (brown?) tunics, and looked past them
(down at) the city, and the (temples around) the

---

[2] Today's Elba.

[3] The Aventine is one of the seven hills on which Rome was
built. The homes of the poor were located at its foot, and the
splendid homes on the hilltop were those of the rich.

Forum.[4] Mother wore gold earrings and was always beautiful and (fragrant), with [1 l] saluted her and turned to stare at (her). Mother would smile at (people) she knew and it (seemed) to me that all of (Rome) smelled like Mama. Once when we [2 wds] the Capitoline,[5] where [1–2 ls] "No, Questus, child, not there. Is it not enough that [10 ls]

7

of the oldest and wealthiest (families) in Rome. But they accumulated even more (property), because during the Civil War, they were among the most ardent [5–6 wds] of (Octavian). Augustus [1–2 ls] (became) consul[6]

---

[4] The Forum (*Romanum*) was Rome's main marketplace, but also its promenade, the venue for public assemblies and a meeting place for friends, where all things possible and impossible were the object of discussion and conjecture.

[5] The Capitoline is another of the hills of Rome, housing its high society. Ovid lived near the Capitoline hilltop, which may explain Proculeia's definitive "No, no, Questus, child, not there," apparently refusing to take her little boy to visit his "uncle" at home.

[6] In the Republic, the consul was the most powerful sovereign bureaucrat of the Roman state. The power of the position diminished in the Empire, but nevertheless remained an important office. The consul presided over the court in a ceremonial chair (*sella curculis*) and had the right to be accompanied by twelve lictors carrying the legendary bundles of birch rods with an axe in their centre, symbolic of power and the ability to punish crimes. His powers included having the final word in capital trials. One of his important privileges was presiding over popular games (*ludi*) and religious festivals.

8

almost always with some of her friends, who kept up
a constant stream of jokes and flatteries to amuse
her. Caecina would just sit there, his hands folded
over his belly, fixing Proculeia with an intense stare,
his eyes tiny in his pudgy face. Once, when father
was holding a banquet for Mar(cus) Sempronius,
mother was called into the kitchen, and Spurius
Avidiacus leaned over to Caecina and whispered
loudly, "Don't be so obvious, undressing her with
your eyes!" That made everyone laugh, but Caecina
flushed and when mother returned and asked what
everyone had found so funny, Manius Tullius said
that Caecina had asked who the "Arachne"[7] was that
mother had spoken of before she was called away.
Then everyone laughed again—all except mother,
who began to explain to Caecina

9

Ventro owned large properties in [5–6 wds] brickworks, and supplied the marble[8] when Augustus

---

[7] Arachne is the skilful weaver from Book 6 of Ovid's
Metamorphoses. Here Caecina reveals his ignorance of Roman
mythology.

[8] Other sections of this text indicate that Caecina was a senator.
It was inappropriate for senators to engage in any activity but
politics and the management of their estates. Brickworks, however,
were considered part of agriculture, so the business-savvy Caecina
bought into brickworks, and later, when Augustus decided to

[2–3 ls] and was said to be wealthier than father. But I say this because when Spurius Caecina used to sit with his hands folded on his belly, mother would sometimes turn to him with some question or other, but I don't believe she ever meant to embarrass him. Caecina always blushed as he answered, though, and he would rock his interlaced fingers up and down, repeatedly up and [1–2 ls] fingers intertwined. Later I often (recalled) that image when I [1 l] to do it so that

From here onward, the quality of much of the manuscript improves, so that some of the fragments consist of longer coherent passages.

10

Baiae.[9] Our fathers both owned villas there, by the sea. Quintus and I used to swim far out from the shore and then back to lie on the sand. I loved Quintus more than anyone else, more than mother, more than Cynthia—I was fond of Cynthia because she was my first lover, but I did not love her. She was too old when she instructed me about how things are done with a woman. Almost twenty-seven.

---

rebuild Rome as the marble centre of the Empire, he acquired the marble business as well.

[9] Baiae was a charming spot on the Bay of Naples, an old site for the summer estates of Rome's elite. There were many baths there, some of them even equipped with libraries.

I loved Quintus, although I never touched him. Our love was like that (described) by Plato[10] [5 ls] one of the most profound perceptions of beauty [3 ls]. Like me, he also had a lover. Her name was Nerva, and, because she played the cithara nicely, she had no other duties at home except to play during banquets. But I was the one he loved. We were the closest of friends. We were no more than fifteen or sixteen years old, still wearing red stripes on our tunics.[11] Both of us were studying law—I with Gaius Aquatius Sulla—and preparing for the

---

[10] Questus is referring to the famous passage in Plato's *Symposium*, which is often interpreted to mean that the love among young men recommended by the philosopher was homosexual love. Even today, an intense emotional relationship is common among youths, which is characterized by Plato as moving "from one to two and from two to all beautiful bodies, from beautiful bodies to beautiful activities, from activities to beautiful sciences, and finally from sciences to that science, which is the science of nothing other than beauty itself, in order that one may finally know what beauty is, itself." Clearly, this passage is open to a variety of interpretations, which is why Questus stresses that he "never touched him" and that their love was an experience of "perceptions of beauty."

[11] The insignia of Roman teenagers comprised two stripes leading down the tunic from both shoulders. The tunic was a shirt, knee-length for boys, ankle-length for girls, worn under the *pallium* (cloak).

tirocinium.[12] Unlike Quintus, I was bored with the law, and the prospect of two years in some office and then three years in the army filled me with despair. And I told Quintus about how my uncle Ovid had quit the *tirocinium* and never went into the army. Instead he attached himself to Messala[13] [2–3 wds] (nothing) but write poetry.

"But you couldn't write poetry," said Quintus, "and speaking of your uncle's poetry, yesterday in the

---

[12] The *tirocinium* was the system whereby well-born (patrician) youths were prepared for a career in politics. It had four levels: (1) apprenticeship with some eminent lawyer and rhetorician; (2) *tirocinium fori*, one or two years' study of administration, including the legal system; (3) *tirocinium militiae*, military training, which youths generally underwent on a divisional staff where one of their relatives was serving; and (4) a subordinate post in state administration, to be held until the age of twenty-seven, when the student could become a *quaestor*, a magistrate, the first step in a career that could culminate in a senatorship. This preparatory course of study, known as *cursus honorum*, took about ten years of a young man's life. Unwillingly, but at the wish of his father, Questus suffered through the whole of his *cursus honorum*, unlike Ovid, who dropped out as early as the *tirocinium fori* to become a professional poet.

[13] Marcus Valerius Messala Corvinus was one of the most colourful figures in Rome of the day, a successful soldier and politician, but also a champion and patron of poets, one way or another ensuring them a comfortable existence.

bath, I was reading his new book, the *Amores*.[14] Wow!" I admitted that I only read poetry when it was absolutely necessary, and that I had not looked into this work. Quintus jumped up, declaring that I didn't know what I was missing, and that we should rectify the situation immediately. "To the baths!" he exclaimed, and off we went.

In the library there, we borrowed the work, which was beautifully encased in yellow leather. The librarian remarked with a smirk that the collection could be useful to us young men; we wouldn't have to waste time getting lessons from female slaves. I snapped at him that we had long since graduated from that school, and that our interest in the book arose solely from our love of poetry. The librarian chuckled, but we paid no attention to him. We were in a hurry to get to the pool. I did not give his behaviour a second thought at the time, though later I [approx. 10 ls]

in the Forum," whispered Quintus, "they talk about the Emperor doing it with your uncle Ovid's first wife, Racilia. That was why he divorced her, because the story got back to him. Of course, he couldn't very well put that in a poem, and in his latest work, *he* is the one doing the cuckolding."

---

[14] *Amores* (Loves) was Ovid's collection of five books of erotic poems, revolving around the heroine Corinna. It was probably published in 15 B.C. In response to its great success, Ovid reworked it in 9 B.C. and shortened it to three books, and in this form it became the equivalent of today's best-seller.

"Really? Cuckolding the Emperor?" I asked. Quintus glanced around nervously. [2 cols]

We thought better of it and returned to our reading, that is, Quintus read aloud to me.

"By Jove!" I said, interrupting him. "I had no idea that poems were written about such things!" and appreciatively, I repeated the lines he had just read: *"and as for Corinna, in one short night I remember, she made me perform nine times, no less.'*[15] I have to say, this kind of poetry is definitely not boring."

"Listen on," said Quintus. *"But still my member lay there, an embarrassing case of premature death—"*

"Let me see that!" I grabbed the book. Now I was the one reading aloud to him. At all the lewder passages, Quintus would lick his lips greedily, and the two of us kept breaking out in giggles.

II

because father had always been his staunch friend and ally during the Civil War, in command of [2 ls]

---

[15] Questus is quoting from *Amores* 3.7, which is also the source of the subsequent quotation about the poet's member lying there, "an embarrassing case of premature death." There has been considerable speculation about the actual identity of the Corinna of the poems: according to some, she was simply a figment of Ovid's fantasy; according to others, she was Ovid's first wife. Of course, assuming the veracity of the Questus manuscript, she was in fact Proculeia, wife to Gaius Firmus and mother to Questus.

When Octavian became Emperor, father was away so much that in truth I hardly knew him: he served in several campaigns. When he was at home he was in the state administration as Augustus's praetorian legate.[16] In that capacity, he had direct access to the Emperor and was invited to the banquets that Augustus held from time to time. These occasions were far less frequent than the parties thrown by senators or upstart freedmen, and Augustus's house on the Palatine was smaller and much less ostentatious than those of others, such as our neighbour Gnaeus Salvidienus Alba, who was always boasting about his private bath with mosaic floors of Phrygian marble, inlaid with pink marble from Chios.

I first attended one of the Emperor's banquets soon after I assumed my *toga virilis*.[17] Father and I had just had a huge row over my announcement that I had no intention of taking up a political career, and I really didn't want to go, but father forced me to.

---

[16] One legate was appointed by the Emperor for each province (with a few exceptions), and the commanders (*legati*) of all the legions in the province fell under his jurisdiction. In other words, the *legatus Augusti* was the head man in the province, with numerous opportunities for lining his pockets.

[17] The *toga virilis* was the white toga of manhood, worn by adult Roman males. This pinpoints Questus's age at the time of the Emperor's banquet as just over seventeen.

The Emperor's banquet was no more opulent than his quarters. I paid no attention to what I was eating. I stuck close to my mother, who had taken my side against my father in the argument, but I didn't dare hope that she would be admitted to the Emperor's reception hall after the meal. That, I knew, was normally an all-male affair, except for the Empress, who sometimes joined her husband.

She—the Empress Livia—was reclining on a couch beside my mother's, at the women's table. My mother looked young enough to be her granddaughter. I kept glancing at her; I had a knot in my stomach at the thought of being left with my father after the banquet, but I felt, as always, proud of my mother, Proculeia; she was as lovely as Aphrodite, and it seemed to me that the entire banquet hall was redolent of her perfume, the fragrance of Rome that I remembered from those days long past when we went on our outings in the litter. Back then her fragrance had seemed to transform the stink of fish from the stalls behind the Forum, just as now at the Emperor's banquet it disguised the stenches from the kitchen. It occurred to me to wonder if I was not something like Oedipus,[18] but I immediately rejected

---

[18] The well-read Questus refers to the Greek myth and Sophoclean tragedy of Oedipus, who married Queen Jocasta, unaware that she was his own mother. When he discovered what he had done, he put out his eyes, and Jocasta killed herself.

the idea. I was simply *primus inter pares*[19] in the
ranks of my mother's admirers. She was a true Roman
matron; lovely and smiling, she kept her ardent
entourage laughing at her witty remarks, and admiring
the lines of poetry she recited—poetry I wasn't
familiar with, which made me feel rather ignorant.
But that was all. She was a paragon of chastity;
Augustus would have pointed to her as his example
when he proclaimed his law against adultery.[20]

Against all expectations the Emperor did invite
Proculeia to join us, while the Empress vanished,
presumably to some drawing-room. Augustus
collapsed into a massive chair. Father, mother, and I
sat on small seats at his feet. The Emperor had
recently celebrated—privately, within the circle of his
odd family—his sixty-fifth birthday. He did not look
well. He kept clearing his throat, and whenever his
eyes rested on me, he looked annoyed, as if he were
thinking, "This kid is a real pain in the ass."

Father started right in complaining about me.

---

[19] First among equals. During the Republic, this designation
referred to the premier man in the state, the leader of the
Senate. Augustus appropriated the title and thenceforth it was
automatically associated with the position of Emperor, and
included among his many titles.

[20] The *lex Julia de adulteris coercendis*. Under it, a wife's adultery
was grounds for divorce, but the man had to act on it within sixty
days. If he failed to do so, he was obliged to remain with his
unfaithful wife.

After just a year of the *tirocinium*, I refused to continue with the *cursus honorum*, etc., etc. Jupiter only knew what I intended to do with my life. It was a time-honoured tradition in our family, he said, the firstborn son to follow in his father's footsteps. Never before had there been a firstborn, not to mention an only son, who had refused to do so. No such black sheep had ever existed in all our kin, as far back as memory reaches, blah, blah, blah. [1 col] He was scowling and looking at Proculeia as he spoke, but my mother was staring straight ahead. I was struck again by her resemblance to a white marble Aphrodite [3–4 ls] write poetry too, Questus?"

"No, I don't." I shook my head.

The Emperor did not take his eyes off me, eyes that were still telling me what a pain I was. "So, what *are* your plans, Questus?" he asked.

"I'm going to—" I began, and then quickly corrected myself, "I want—" Here an expression of derision appeared on the Emperor's face. "—I'd like to—" I stammered, feeling the blood rush to my cheeks "—to invent—for the army—"

But before I get another word out, father burst in with "Toys! Almost eighteen-years-old and he thinks up toys! What is the army supposed to do with that?" He motioned to his slave, Sentris, who left the room. We sat in silence for a moment. Then the Emperor started coughing and a slave passed him a goblet with something that was not wine. I suddenly knew that my cause was lost. Sentris came running back with a satchel, from which he [about 10 ls] but stopped when [2 wds] slipped out [2 ls] no sympathy from that quarter, which wasn't a surprise.

"Well," said the Emperor, rising from his chair. We stood too. "Obey your father, Questus," he said peremptorily. "You are young and healthy, and luckily you don't write poetry. In two years, you'll enter military service. You'll serve with your uncle, Sempronius Severus, on the staff of Germanicus. There you [1 wd] learn more of military life than you [1 l]. The matter is closed."

So that was that. We all bowed, and the Emperor turned around and left us.

We did not speak on the way home. The thought that I had to attend the execution of that murderer[21]—I couldn't even think of his name

12

sat motionless, except for mindlessly rocking his folded fingers up and down on his fat belly. With a fine chisel, Racimachos picked away a bit of stone here, smoothed a spot with pumice there, until a true-to-life Caecina emerged from the marble. All of his several chins were represented, as was the wart on his left cheek; a wreath of marble hair formed a narrow frame for the bald pate that Racimachos was in the process of polishing. At last he stepped away from it. "Done," he said.

---

[21] One of the duties of a youth in his *tirocinium* was to occasionally oversee executions.

Caecina stood up and walked around the bust to look at it from the front. His expression saddened. "It's very nice, very nice," he said. "Only busts like that used to … how can I put it? They used to resemble the person—"

Racimachos interrupted him. "That is no longer the fashion," he said. "Take the latest bust of Caesar. Or the one of Sempronius Severus. Their baldness is there for all to see, Caecina. Busts that make everyone look like Apollo have gone out of style."[22]

"You must be right, Racimachos," said Caecina, "but—"

The sculptor broke in again. "Or even better, take Pompey. He also has a double chin, and his cheeks are clear evidence of his fondness for food. This is my style, Caecina. If it's not to your liking, find another artist. But no first-rate sculptor in Rome today will portray you the old-fashioned way. He'd be a laughing stock among his colleagues. Of course, if you insist on looking like Apollo," Racimachos grinned and, with an obvious glance to Caecina's

---

[22] Greek sculptors who settled in Rome at the close of the Republic and on into the Empire turned their backs on the earlier trend of portrait busts that idealized the model. The best-known example of their sculpture is a realistic bust depicting the sardonic face of the quintessential gourmand, Gnaeus Pompeius Magnus, one of Rome's greatest politicians and military leaders. In part responsible for the Civil War, he fought against Caesar; defeated, he fled to Egypt, where he was murdered.

showy *toga candida*,[23] continued, "hire yourself some Academic hack. I have no intention of making a fool of myself."

"Oh, no," Caecina responded hurriedly. "Of course I don't want to look like Apollo. I'd be laughed at as much as you would. It's just that—" Pointing a tentative finger at the beautifully sculpted wart, he timidly asked, "if you could possibly ..."

"Everyone who knows you knows your wart. Why hide it?" said Racimachos. Caecina capitulated, sighing, and looked so crestfallen that I felt sorry for him.

He looked over at me. "What do you think, Questus?"

"A perfect likeness, Spurius," I said. "Racimachos is a master. You look a little like Nexitelos's Hephaestos, except, of course, you're not lame." That seemed to make him feel a bit better; in any case, he didn't ask for any more changes. He was afraid of having a bust that was less than fashionable.

Later on, he and I sat together on a block of marble from one of his quarries, watching workers placing the hewn slabs side by side, fitting them perfectly one to the next. That really interested me. They were applying marble panels to a concrete structure, so that the temple of the divine Julius would gleam in the sun like Caecina's toga.

---

[23] *Toga candida* means "white toga"; the fabric's whiteness was artificially enhanced by the application of chalk.

All of a sudden, Caecina said to me, "If Racimachos were to sculpt your mother, he could do it just as he did me—I mean, an exact likeness—and she would still look like Aphrodite."

I knew what he wanted to hear. "Yes, mother is certainly beautiful." He nodded, and we sat again in silence. The wall, now completely encased in marble, glowed in the sunlight till it hurt the eyes. Caecina sighed, and sighed again, then finally came out with what was on his mind. "You know, Questus, if you had a sister ..." he hesitated, and quickly added, "an older sister, of course, I...." The rest remained unspoken, but I knew the trend of his thoughts. He did look like a very unattractive and fleshy Hephaestos, but he was one of the ten wealthiest men in Rome. That wouldn't help him much with Proculeia, but he would have been quite a catch for any sister I might have had. He gave another heartfelt sigh, and we fell silent again. The workers were positioning a rectangular slab between two others. As it fell neatly into place, he asked, "How long has it been, Questus, since I first came to your place in Baiae? Has it been ten years? Your father was serving with the army at Ilva. Remember that silly little thing I brought you?"

"Yes, I remember. It flew away into the sea. And I also remember [2 ls] that father, away at war, might some day not return from one of his campaign. Was that possibility on Caecina's mind? If it were—but surely he couldn't be thinking—I glanced over at him, at his chins, which Racimachos had given their full due, at his jowls, which, even more than Pompey's, attested to his love of good food, and dismissed the idea. I wanted to cheer him up, and although I knew he didn't want to talk about her, I couldn't think of anything else to say, and foolishly asked, "Have you seen mother's new amber necklace, the one Uncle Ovid brought her from Greece?"

Another tumult of sighs. Poor Caecina. "Oh, yes. You know, your uncle [2 cols] thought of my pretty little Cynthia, and all of a sudden, like those slabs of gleaming marble

13

is like what I hate most about work in an office. Except here no one knows in advance who will be the executioner and who—"

Father interrupted me, scolding. "Stop talking like [1 col]

He looked around the arena. At least half the people there were women, all squealing like maniacs. I couldn't help making a face. Father noticed, and his face grew flushed with anger.

"Even so!" he snapped. "These are slaves and criminals. It is generous of the Emperor to give them a chance [2–3 wds] equal against equal."

Down in front of us, a *retiarius* was fleeing. He had lost his net and all he had left was a trident. A *mirmillo*[24] followed, carrying a sword and shield and

---

[24] The *retiarius* and the *mirmillo* were two types of gladiators: the *retiarius* fought with a net and trident, using the first to entangle

wearing a helmet. I turned away from the spectacle as father ranted, "The greatness of Rome is in battle! Our army—"

I stopped listening. When our armies fought, it was not a fight to the death for the entertainment of the proles. I felt like telling him that it wasn't my fault that I preferred the comedies of Plautus to scenes of butchery in the arena. And that if I wanted to see a performance that ended in murder, I'd go to a tragedy by Lucius Sempronius. But I held my tongue, realizing that if I said what I thought it would only pour oil on the fire. Father was almost shouting, but I ignored him. The crowd in the arena suddenly roared, so I didn't even have to look: the chase was over. From the corner of my eye I could see the Emperor raise his fist with the thumb pointing downward. Then I heard a penetrating shriek, which, of course, was almost drowned out by the cheers and hurrahs. To his credit, father had stopped shouting.

"Never fear, father," I said. "What I promised, I

---

his opponent and the second to finish him off (on the Emperor's command). It is clear from the scene described that an unfortunate *retiarius* who had lost his net would have been at the mercy of the *mirmillo*, who was armed with a sword, a long shield, and a large helmet.

SCROLL II

FRAGMENT

I

clearly Bato had superiority in numbers, and from
the experience of having once been allied with us
had some knowledge of how the legions of Rome
wage war.[1] But he seemed to have forgotten all that.

---

[1] This fragment describes the battle in about 8 B.C. for the
Andetrium fortress near Salonae, capital of the province of
Illyricum on the Adriatic coast. Bato, the commander of the
Dalmatians, met with defeat there at the hands of an army under
Tiberius (later emperor) and Julius Caesar Germanicus, a highly
capable general and Tiberius's celebrated adopted son. His extreme
popularity aroused the envy of both Tiberius and Livia, wife of
Augustus. When later, on 10 October, A.D. 19, Germanicus died
suddenly in Syria, Tiberius and Livia (as well as several others)
were suspected of having had him poisoned.

This fragment is also an eyewitness report of how the Roman
war machine functioned, and as such, calls for some detailed
background.

The basic unit of the Roman battle formation was the
maniple (*manipulus*), comprising two centuries (*centuria*). Three
maniples formed a cohort (*cohors*). Every century consisted of
between sixty and seventy men (in earlier times one hundred),
with a centurion (*centurio*) in command. The foremost man in

He tried to maintain his battle line along its entire
breadth, from [2–3 wds] to the sea, which inevitably
stretched it very thin. I turned to Germanicus and
caught him smiling. Then he gave the command to

---

the field was the *primus pilus*, the senior centurion, commander
of the first century of the first cohort.

The usual Roman battlefield order (*triplex acies*) is described
as a three-row chequerboard (*quincunx*), one to two miles long,
consisting of three ranks of maniples, each maniple situated
behind a gap separating two maniples in the line ahead.

The battle was launched by light-armed skirmishers supported
by a light cavalry (*velites*). After the initial brief skirmish, these
withdrew through the gaps between the maniples lined up and
waiting behind them. Then the first line of maniples, the *hastati*,
advanced to within about fifty yards of the enemy, broke into a
run, and at about thirty yards hurled their javelins (*pilum*) at the
enemy. Then, holding up their shields and brandishing their
swords, they attacked. They penetrated the enemy line through
openings where enemy soldiers had fallen and, now relieved of
their javelins, fought with their swords, going after the enemy's
unprotected legs and arms. At that point, the second line of
maniples, the *principes*, were preparing to attack. When the
hastati tired, they withdrew between the advancing maniples of
the *principes*, who in turn charged the enemy with a new assault.

These *principes* were the most seasoned and skilled of the
legionaries, and as a rule, debilitated the enemy, usually deciding
the outcome of the battle. If not, then the third line of maniples,
the *triarii*, moved into action. They had been kneeling in the rear
with shields raised and spears levelled, watching for any wavering
among the first two waves of offense. At the decisive moment,

attack, and Gnaeus Sempronius galloped off to deliver his orders to the first centurion of the first company of the first cohort, and the [3 wds] was on the move.

It was then that I first thought of the perfect word

---

when victory was in sight, they advanced to finish off the dazed enemy troops, who were thoroughly intimidated by the spectacle of line upon daunting line of fresh warriors assaulting them. Moreover, the legionary machine was flanked by auxiliary cavalry and light-armed allied troops. And of all this to the thunder of brasses, the Roman tubas.

The functioning of this "machine," literally a killing machine, can be better visualized if its action shown in illustration—which I shall now attempt to do:

★ Triarii ● Hastati

■ Principes ▼ Velites

ATTACK PHASE I

The light-armed *velites* advance to launch the assault with skirmishes, and then retreat through the gaps between the maniples of *hastati*, *principes*, and *triarii*:

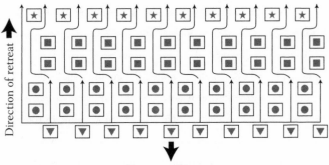

Direction of retreat

Direction of assault

to describe the legions' order of battle. Impressed, I observed how the skirmishers streamed back between the maniples of the first, second, and third lines, moving through the gaps like water flowing through some multi-channel aqueduct; I saw how the legionaries of

---

ATTACK PHASE 2

The rear centuries of the *hastati* move to between the forward ones, creating a solid line to advance, fling their javelins, and rush at the enemy with shields raised and swords drawn:

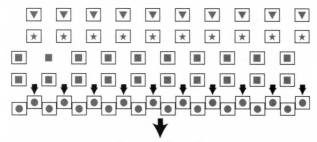

direction of assault

ATTACK PHASE 3

The *hastati* split back into their individual centuries and retreat through the gaps between the advancing *principes* to become the rear line:

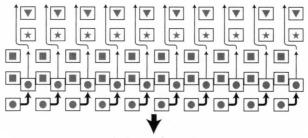

direction of assault

the first wave flung their javelins in unison at Bato's forward line, so close now that almost all of them hit their mark; how the *hastati* followed up the javelins by rushing forward with their swords, slashing into the ranks of Bato's dazed troops. I was struck with a strong sense of some significance in what I was seeing, a significance specific to me. I shivered not with fear, but with some sort of elation. The dreadful

---

ATTACK PHASE 4

As soon as the *hastati* have moved through, the rear units of the *principes* advance to form a similar, closed line, and attack.

The enemy finds itself faced with fresh, new troops, without the break they would have had if the forward lines had simply turned and retreated and the ones behind them had been obliged to go all the way around them:

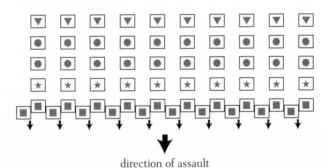

direction of assault

ATTACK PHASE 5

When the *principes* show signs of tiring, they too retreat through the gaps between the spear-brandishing *triarii*, who advance behind their shields to form another closed rank. The already debilitated enemy must now deal with a third wave of fresh and vigorous warriors. This is the phase that generally decides the battle.

blasts of the *tubas* seemed to grow faint as I looked at the backs of the *tubicinis* behind the third rank of men, who were kneeling, spears extended, presenting their shields. Suddenly, instead of the battle, I saw the solution that would allow for the transfer of the rotational force to [about ½ col] second line was now flowing back through the gaps between maniples,

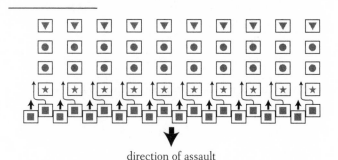

direction of assault

ATTACK PHASE 6

The *triarii* now finish off what is left of the enemy, or, should their opponents prove especially resilient, launch the multi-phase battle again.

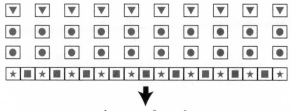

direction of assault

I trust the above depiction of the largely *mechanical* Roman system of combat shows how the precision of that military machine could have inspired Questus and sparked his imagination to arrive at his invention.

and the third line was rising, closing ranks and charging forward through the breach, hurling their javelins and striking out with their swords at the lines of the stunned enemy. Bato's men apparently mustered a brave defense, because Germanicus had to call up a fourth wave, but once again, all the components of the legion worked like—once again, I thought of that word, which expressed so well the [3–4 ls] the auxiliary cavalry joined the fray, and Bato's crumbling army

2

when you are released from the army. When will that be?"

"This autumn," said Lucius Agricola. "I've already served three extra years."

"Where would you like to have your estate?"[2]

He shook his head. "I don't want a farm. I want a workshop, and to stay with my trade."

"In Rome?"

"No, probably in Lugdunum. I like it there. They have a new amphitheatre, lots of taverns, and plenty of space. No three-storey buildings, and streets so narrow that if you stand in the middle of them and spread your arms, you can touch the walls of the houses on both sides."

---

[2] Veterans of Rome's army were given land and became farmers. Once all the land in Italy was gone, they settled for the most part around permanent military installations such as Lugdunum (today's Lyon), which was Agricola's choice.

I fell silent and watched him deftly repairing a suit
of strip armor.[3] It belonged to a legionary whose
name I could see inscribed on the inner surface of a
shield[4] that was also awaiting repair. *Platus*, it said, *of
the company of Centurion Galobladus.*

Crunching a hard biscuit,[5] Platus himself sat
nearby on a rock next to the pile of ammunition that
stood waiting for the onagers.[6] I knew him. He was
an old soldier, apparently not too far from retiring.
Undoubtedly a *princeps*, and, judging from his almost

---

[3] Strip armor (*lorica segmentata*) was made of horizontal metal
segments fastened to a leather backing. This type of armor was
in use at the time of the early emperors.

[4] This was a common method whereby legionaries identified
their personal equipment to ensure it would not go astray.

[5] A basic component of a soldier's field rations, biscuits (*bucce-
lata*) resembled what was later known in the navy as hardtack.

[6] The heavy artillery of the Roman army, used well into the
Middle Ages, was the onager, a one-armed catapult weighing
about two tons, capable of heaving stone projectiles or lead balls
a distance of some four hundred yards. It required nine men,
four to a side and the gunner. When the machine was aimed, the
gunner would take a strong hammer and strike out the bolt,
which released the pole to fly forward and hurl the projectile.
Each of the ten cohorts of a legion had such an onager. While
lighter catapults (*scorpiones*) and heavier ones (*ballistae*) were
also used, the onager was standard equipment. The weapon
which hit the barrel with the flaming liquid would have probably
been a *scorpio*, not the onager as Questus thought. It is unlikely
that the massive onager would have such precision of aim.

totally destroyed gear, a dauntless warrior. One of
Bato's soldiers had split his shield almost in two with
his battle axe.

Lucius Agricola was now replacing the broken
metal segments of the breast plate with brand new
ones, skilfully attaching them to the leather backing,
brandishing his hammer to rivet each segment to
the base on his anvil. It was a pleasure to watch
him work.

"So you don't like Rome?" I asked him.

Agricola shook his head. Lifting the repaired
armor with both hands, he signaled to Platus with
a jerk of his chin. When the old soldier stood up—
and up and up—he was a veritable giant. Agricola
helped him into his cuirass and fastened the straps
on either side.

"Would you live in Rome if you had steady work,
better paid than anything you could get in
Lugdunum?"

"It would have to be damn well paid for me to put
up with the stink of Rome."

"How about Baiae? It's not exactly in Rome. A
holiday town by the sea. We have a villa there."

Wearing his armor, Platus went back to his rock.
Agricola picked up the shield and scowled at it from
under the bushy eyebrows in his senatorially clean-
shaven face. "Have them issue you a new one,
Platus," he said. "I could repair it, but not in time.
Germanicus won't delay much longer." He pointed to
the nearby fortress in the morning sun, with onagers
lining up around it.

"All right," said Platus, getting up again. There was a deep scar on his left thigh, but he walked straight, without any sign of a limp. I stared after him. The new segments of his armor shone like silver.

"Holiday town, you say," mused (Agricola)

3

(with)in earshot of Salonae. All twenty onagers of both our legions were operating and the maniples were falling in for the attack. I have always been fascinated by how the siege engines work. I watched from the command post on the hill as four men loaded a flaming projectile onto the onager nearest us. Then another struck the handle with a mallet, popping out the pin. The huge arm of the engine sprang up, slammed into a slot on the forward cross-beam, and catapulted the fiery projectile toward the Andetrium fortress. The flame flew over the wall and disappeared. I turned to look at Germanicus, who was just raising his hand. He signaled, the trumpets sounded, and the maniples launched the attack.

"Questus!" Sempronius Severus was calling to me. I ran over and he handed me a thin scroll. "For Laetitius."

4

Laetitius Frappus Prominculus's observation post, which the tribune had moved up to just outside shooting distance from the fortress. A large battering ram had been pushed over to the fortress wall, and two ranks of legionaries were rocking it back and forth, protected by a slanted leather roof. On the parapet above them, two men were bouncing a barrel, preparing to pour a flaming liquid down on the men. All of a sudden the barrel burst apart, the two men vanished behind the parapet, and a bit of the blazing liquid fell on the roof, spattering tiny flames over the armor of the men working the ram. Of course! I realized. The onager, and dead on target. Now nothing could stop them from breaching the stone wall.

I leapt from my horse. Laetitius Frappus turned towards me, but before I could take a step a boulder came flying from the fortress, knocking my legs out from under me. I fell flat. At first I felt no pain, just a brutal impact, as if someone had smashed me across the shins with a club. But as I lay on the ground the pain began to assert itself. A centurion bent over me and I handed him the scroll from Sempronius Severus; he took it away. For a while I controlled myself, and when a howl of pain rose in my throat, I was able to stifle that disgraceful expression of weakness. A column of smoke rose beyond the fortress wall, then flames shot up, and there was a huge crash and shouting as the legionaries with the ram succeeded in breaking through. All around me, *principes* were running toward the breach in the wall, and others were raising scaling ladders on either side of the gaping hole. A new barrel appeared on the parapet, but the men at the onagers again demonstrated their excellent aim. Before the

Dalmatians could tip the barrel, a projectile smashed into it exploding its contents into a relatively harmless rain of spattering fire. The only one hurt was a legionary who had just started up one of the ladders. He screamed and rolled around on the ground but another immediately took his place on the ladder. Trumpets sounded from somewhere behind me. The *tubicinis* must have been running toward the opening in the wall, sounding their horns at full blast. A verse by Ennius flashed into my mind, the only one of the poems Claudius Menicius Paullus made us read that had stayed with me, in which the poet successfully captured the sound of trumpets: "*At tuba terribili sonitu taratantara dixit.*"[7] Something about those words struck me as funny, but suddenly everything grew foggy. I just barely realized that I was being loaded onto a litter, and then I was in limbo.

I came to in the antechamber of the hospital in Salonae. All around me I could hear the stifled moans of men trying to maintain their dignity and

---

[7] A line from *Annales*, a work by the Roman historian and dramatist Quintus Ennius (239–169 B.C.), which captures in hexameter the history of Rome beginning with Aeneas's flight from Troy to the time of the author. The work consisted of eighteen volumes, but only some six hundred lines of it have been preserved, for the most part fragmentary and lacking context, and that only thanks to subsequent poets who quoted Ennius in their own works.

refrain from shameful, unmanly outbursts, and the agonized howls of others, who were beyond any such concerns.

The physician[8] was bending over me and exclaiming cheerily, "Questus, my boy! They really gave it to you, didn't they?" It was my uncle Valerius Aemilius Saepulus, Proculeia's brother, who had made a name for himself with a book on the straightening of broken bones. Now he set to work, giving a practical demonstration of how it is done, and although I did my best to maintain a manly silence, or to moan as quietly as I could, I

5

raining, a dice game was going on in the corner when Valerius Aemilius appeared and sat beside me on the cot. "How are you doing, Questus? No more itchy skin?" He indicated the bandages that made my legs look like two shapeless bundles.

I shook my head, but before I could say a word, one of the dice-playing centurions shouted, "Don't worry, doctor, he can get it up already. Last night it ..."

"Shut up, Burrus!" I snapped. To the legionaries

---

[8] Permanent garrisons had well-equipped hospitals with qualified doctors (*medici ordinarii*), many of them *equites*, as Proculeia's brother Valerius Aemilius would apparently have been. In this fragment we also learn Proculeia's family name, Aemilia, and her *cognomen*, Saepuli, which she shared with her brother and her father.

this reaction was a huge joke. Valerius Aemilius smiled too, and I [about 5 ls] slowly unwound the bandage, looking at what he was uncovering with what looked to me like a lascivious smile, as if he were undressing a woman. My leg emerged, livid and discoloured, from the bandages. He bent over it, gently stroking it with his long fingers. I could see a pattern of red drops on the top of his bald head, though not from any wound of his own: blood must have spattered on him when he was taking over a newcomer in the antechamber, and he hadn't bothered to wipe it off. He looked up and declared happily, "You aren't out of the woods yet, Questus." Once again, he set to work, torturing me.

From the corner, Burrus repeated his successful joke: "But he can get it up already!"

This time it was Aemilius who told him to shut up, and added, "What about you? Can you get it up? You've been here a month, so I have my doubts. How about letting me examine you?"

Once again, the legionaries found this repartee hilarious. My jovial uncle had by now finished putting a new dressing on my leg. Rising, he said, "Large measures of wine will do your wound no harm at all," and moved on to the next room where three more patients lay recovering from amputations.

Lying back again with nothing to do, I let my thoughts wander. Memories flooded in and—the gods know why—one clear recollection floated up out of that confused current. I suddenly remembered Cynthia's face as she entertained me with a story about the Emperor. "When will you marry again?" he had asked Ovid, and the poet, frowning, cast him a glance so peevish that it bordered on extreme disrespect for His Majesty. By now Cynthia was giggling. "Augustus likes to pretend he is the mildest of men, but he can be very malicious," she said. "He quickly turned to Proculeia and asked in an innocent voice, 'And how is your baby doing, Aemilia?' Ovid was turning purple, a nice senatorial shade of purple. Proculeia raised her head defiantly and—"

"Wait," I interrupted her. "I don't get it. Where is the malice in that?"

"Why, Augustus was pretending not to know about his marital predicament," said Cynthia, and suddenly her face turned red.

"What predicament? Ovid divorced Racilia a long time ago, and he hasn't remarried. Why is it malicious to mention that?"

"You mean, you don't know?" Cynthia looked embarrassed, but also astonished.

"Don't know what?" Just then footsteps sounded from outside, father was returning from the senate. "Tell me!" But Cynthia had jumped up and was leaving my bedroom in a hurry, throwing her stola over her naked body as she went.

Now, thinking back, it all suddenly fell into place. Could she possibly have meant—? No, no, total nonsense. But then another memory swam up out of the hazy tide of my thoughts. Quintus and I were in the pool at Baiae, reading Ovid's dirty poems, and I asked him [about 1 ½ cols]

6

(Aemilius) Saepulus entering the room less than his usual jolly self. "I bring sad tidings, Questus. Your mother says she sent word to you months ago, but this letter arrived from Rome only today, because of the Bato chaos. I regret to tell you that your father, Gaius Firmus, is dead."

"Oh," I said. I felt no grief; in fact I was almost pleased, because hearing of it this late meant I would not have to attend a funeral ceremony in Rome. "When did it happen?"

"Three days before the *nones* of May,"[9] said Aemilius. "Almost half a year ago. How old would he have been?"

I was unwilling to admit ignorance, so I said he was sixty. I thought that was probably about right.

"Hmm," said Valerius. "You seem relatively unaffected, Questus. Not so your mother. I also received a letter from Sixtus Vernius, who says that Proculeia was shocked and inconsolable."

"Well, Mother is a proper Roman matron. Of course she knew how to behave. How did Vernius

---

[9] The Romans divided each month in three parts. The days that marked the divisions were: the *calendae*, the first day of the month; the *nones*, which fell on the seventh day of the month in March, May, July, and October and on the fifth in the rest of the months; and the *ides*, the thirteenth day of all the months except March, May, July, and October, when it fell on the fifteenth. So three days before the *nones* of May would have been 4 May.

come to write you about it?" I asked.

"They were close allies in the Senate, of course."

"I never knew that," I said.

Valerius seemed to hide a smile. "There is much you don't know about your father ..."

I didn't care. I shrugged.

"But Vernius's letter contains more sad news: Augustus has banished Ovid to exile."

"Why?" I was aghast. This news upset me far more than the word of my father's passing. Exile was a heavy punishment and Ovid would be miserable anywhere but Rome. "What was his crime?"

"His poems, of course. After all, Augustus is the epitome of morality." Aemilius smirked again, this time not over me and my supposed ignorance. "Ovid's guidelines on how to cuckold a husband displeased the Emperor. He has also sent Julia into exile for marital infidelity. I mean the imperial granddaughter. Her mother has already been in exile for ten years, for the same offense: not saving the bliss of her holy shrine for her husband."

"But—" I was bewildered. "Those poems came out at least nine years ago!"

"Not quite. Eight years ago," said Valerius. "But apparently Augustus only read them recently. He must have been royally enraged, because he also issued execution orders for

The remainder of the scroll is destroyed. The text continues on the next, the third, scroll.

SCROLL III

1

but Proculeia just smiled sadly and shook her head.
"I don't entirely understand [about 3 wds] functions,"
said Agricola, "but Questus is brilliant [2 ls] (never)
tried to." Proculeia stared out to sea, her thoughtful
expression one I had often seen before. Her eyes were
strangely empty. Was she remembering something?
Someone? Or was she just sad? She was sitting on
the terrace and I wondered what was going through
her mind. Since father's death

2

the way to Rome, the memory of my mother's sudden
exclamation came to me over and over. With something like passion, she cried out, "He's taking revenge
on him!" then stopped herself and refused to say any
more. I could not

3

so sad to read. Do you remember, in the library, the
first time we read *The Art of Love*? We had no idea
then that ...." He turned his face away from me. A
reflected ray of sunlight flashed from his equestrian
ring.

4

three conversations, and then, when Caecina told me

5

not really a banquet, only a few people were invited.[1]
Brutus was Quintus's uncle, and knew me through
my mother, who used to borrow books from his size-
able library. In addition to Quintus and me, Brutus
had invited two of his close friends, Curtius Atticus
and Carus. Once we had all exchanged greetings,
Brutus motioned to a slave, who left the room and
quickly returned not with wine, but with five scrolls,
which he distributed among us.

Before we had time to look at them to see what
they were all about, Brutus said, "This may be a little
unusual, but I'd like you all to read these. The wine

---

[1] All of the participants in the literary/political discussion described
here are Ovid's friends. Brutus was his literary representative and
editor, and Ovid had dedicated numerous poems to him, in *Tristia*
as well as in *Epistulae ex Ponto*. By profession a lawyer, Brutus
was apparently one of the poet's most devoted compeers. Others
included Curtius Atticus and Carus. Not much is known of them,
except what Ovid says of them in *Tristia*, *Epistulae ex Ponto*, and
elsewhere (Poem 9 in Book 1 of *Amores*, where loving is compared
to military service, is dedicated to Curtius). Carus was tutor to
the sons of Germanicus, and he is known as the author of a
poem about Hercules. All these poets lived on the periphery of
the Roman social elite, admiring its grandeur but not a part of it.
Today, they might be referred to as middle-class intellectuals.

will be served in a few minutes. This is the next, the
twelfth, epistle from our friend on the Pontic shore, a
small book.[2] I want you all to tell me what you [about
10 cols] brought wine and mussels, and Simeria, one
of Brutus's slaves, took up her harp and played a sad
Greek melody.

Brutus turned an amused eye to me and Quintus.
"I'm interested in what you young people think of the
book. I know, Questus," he was chortling by now,
"that you don't care much for poetry, but that's exactly
why I want your opinion—a barbarian's view, so to
speak. So suspend your distaste for a while. Perhaps
a little Setian wine[3] will help." He gestured to a slave,
who topped up my cup. "This wine is appropriate to
the occasion—even the divine Augustus likes it." He
was still laughing, and it made his fat belly shake. His
merriment was hardly appropriate to the occasion, I
thought. Ovid had surely not sent anything from
Tomis to inspire mirth.

Indeed, he had not. It was a lament—the latest of
a series. *"Books, my unlucky obsession,[4] why do I stay
with you when it was my own talent brought me down?"*
And on and on, not just a mere elegy, but an entire book.

I was barely halfway through it when Curtius put
down his scroll and wiped a tear from his eye. "He

---

[2] Brutus is referring to Book 2 of *Tristia*, which was as long as a
separate Roman book would be.

[3] A wine grown in the immediate vicinity of Rome.

[4] *Tristia*, Book 2, lines 1–2.

is demeaning himself," he declared. "But in that backwoods—"

"Demeaning?" Brutus interjected sarcastically. "I say he's looking for a thrashing!"

I looked over at our host in surprise, his [about 3 ls] *"she deserved no other husband;*[5] *without her, a bachelor existence should have been yours; whom else could you have married?"* After reading this Brutus looked around as if expecting us to agree with him. "And this is supposed to appeal to the divine Augustus?"

We were silent. I found nothing in the verse to offend the Emperor, but of course—

"The way it is, it says nothing," said Carus. He was well known as the most muscular of Rome's poets, but also so dense that you had to repeat a funny story to him three times over, and then count up to a hundred before he got the point.

Affecting surprise, Brutus asked, "You mean you don't know how it was with the Emperor and the Empress?"[6] I started counting, and this time Carus

---

[5] *Tristia*, Book 2, lines 163–164.

[6] Livia had been married to Tiberius Claudius Nero, by whom she had a son, Tiberius, later to become emperor. In 39 B.C., before Octavian became the imperial Augustus, his wife Scribonia bore him a daughter, whereupon he divorced her. A year later, he forced Tiberius Claudius to divorce Livia, whom he immediately married himself, although she was six months pregnant at the time. In fact, Tiberius Claudius even attended the wedding and, in the absence of Livia's father, took the role of the

caught on by the time I reached twenty-three.

"Oh, that," he said. "Yes, of course I know. But Publius doesn't say anything about that."

"That, Carus, is known as the silence that speaks volumes. Or else as irony." I started counting. When I got to thirty-seven, the muscular poet's eyes lit up.

"You may be right, Brutus. Augustus is hardly likely to approve."

"Particularly in the context of a line that comes a little further on." Brutus picked up the scroll and began to recite the words. He had studied Ovid's poem closely, maybe he even knew it by heart. I was not surprised. Brutus was an avid reader of poetry, and for that matter, had edited Ovid [about 5 wds] *a temple—yet the girl with a gift for indulging her vice*[7] *should be kept away from there too: Jove's shrine is sure to remind her just how many girls* Jove *put in the family way.*" Brutus laid significant emphasis on the word "Jove."

Carus looked blank. Curtius got it, but looked sad—because he saw no humour in Ovid's daring, or

---

bride's witness. When Livia gave birth to Drusus, Octavian sent him to his father, and all over Rome people joked that some fortunate people have children only three months after the wedding.

[7] *Tristia*, Book 2, lines 288–290. The reference to Jove is a clear allusion to the fact that the "divine" Augustus used to be a womanizer. The allusion is reinforced by the use in Latin of the word *augustus* in the preceding line, "nothing's more august than a temple."

perhaps saw only his foolhardiness—and remarked, "As if he hadn't had enough already, the poor wretch."

"You said you wanted to hear our opinion," said Quintus. "The opinion of youth."

Brutus turned to me. "Have you anything to say, Questus?"

I shook my head. "Quintus can say it better." I had been taken aback by those lines of the poem as well, but I didn't really want to comment. Of course, Quintus proceeded to recite them:

"*Should you, the Imperial* Princeps, *desert your station to peruse my limping verse?*"[8] Carus fulfilled all expectations by looking baffled, and Quintus, trying to defend the allusion, became angry, though he only showed it by the redness of his face. Even so, I knew what he would have said if Carus had not been twenty years his senior and a high court official.[9]

Simeria began to sing, so we stopped our discussion and listened to the appealing girl and her rather husky voice. As far as mistresses go, Brutus had always had remarkable taste, and in all probability— despite his gigantic belly—other talents as well. The song Simeria was singing, to the caressing accompaniment of her harp, might not have appealed to the Emperor either. At least, he would have claimed not to like it. In any event, Simeria wouldn't have dared to sing it in his august presence. Here, though, no

---

[8] *Tristia*, Book 2, lines 219–220.

[9] He was tutor to the children of Germanicus.

one was offended by the immorality. We were all
sincere admirers of the Emperor, in part because he
had behaved—at least in his youth—according to
mythology, discreetly of course. But then, even Zeus
kept his escapades to himself.

The song ended and Brutus asked, "You, Simeria,
have you read this?"

"No, Brutus," the girl replied. "Would you like me
to? Should I make it into a song?"

Brutus laughed. "Not a bad idea. It would bring
you great success everywhere. In the *frigidarium* at
the spa, someone wrote a single line from the *Art of
Loving* on the wall, maybe the selfsame one that
enraged Augustus. Given the scope of his conquests,
he probably had something like that happen to him
too. Perhaps more than once."

"What line was it?" asked Carus.

Ignoring him, Brutus went on, counting on his
fingers. "Tertulla, Nymphidia, Caenis, Terentilla,
Rufilla, Junia, Salvia Titisenia—to name just the few
I can think of offhand. The Emperor is certainly a
stud. But it can happen even to a stud."

"What line are you talking about?" Carus insisted.

"You tell him, Curtius. Am I mistaken, or did he
dedicate that poem to you?"

"Not that one," said Curtius, "but I know the one
you mean." In a soft voice he spoke the lines for
Carus, and I thought of the afternoon in the (baths)
[about 10 ls] It touches not only on the Emperor's
hypocrisy, but also on his taste as a literary critic,"
said Brutus. "Can you imagine writing something like

that about the founder of the greatest library in Rome? And I quote: *'August One, you'll find you spent massive sums on many such items. You watched them yourself and (bounteous by nature, as always) under-wrote them time and again for the public, [1 l] their staged adulteries. [1 l] the penalty my stuff incurs should be far less'.*"[10] Brutus put down the scroll, and as we read on, he continued, "And to give that kind of advice to the highest judge in the empire? I don't know (how)

6

rose and strode toward me with his arms wide open as if to embrace me. But then he just shook my hand with a certain urgency, grinning at me, flashing his new ivory teeth[11] between his fleshy lips. "Good day

---

[10] *Tristia*, Book 2, lines 510–516. The entire passage will clarify the allusions: "August One, you'll find you spent massive sums on many such items. You watched them yourself and (bounteous by nature, as always) underwrote them time and again for the public, and with those eyes that survey the world, you followed, all cool attention, their staged adulteries. If it's proper to scribble farces that act out such gross matter, the penalty my stuff incurs should be far less." So explicit a critique of the Emperor's hypocrisy could hardly be perceived as being shamefully obsequious.

[11] Roman dentistry was relatively advanced, so that a wealthy man like Caecina could afford to replace his own teeth with a type of prosthetic denture.

to you, Questus, good day. You've come at a very opportune moment!" We sat down to wine and a dish of shrimps. "Proculeia has gone to see Salvia Titisenia,"[12] Caecina continued, "and when she comes home, we'll have a surprise for her!"

I wondered what he was talking about, but didn't ask. Perhaps he meant my presence in his house, but that would hardly surprise my mother. I glanced around the atrium, which he had recently redecorated with magnificent alabaster columns. The cabinets displaying death masks of his forebears[13] looked new, and in fact, they must have been, because the ones he had had before the wedding weren't of ebony, and these were. My gaze flitted down the row of busts, all superb, of Greek marble: Plato, Socrates, Diana, Leda with the Swan, Apollo, Hercules. And before the *tablinum*,[14] on a little dais to the left of a curtain, stood the beautifully sculpted image of the

---

[12] If this is the same Salvia Titisenia referred to by Marc Antony as one of Augustus's paramours (see Antony's letter to Augustus, which I quote in my commentary on page 114), then Proculeia's visiting her is revealing: Questus's mother could have been seeking an ally who would intercede with the Emperor on behalf of an unfortunate former lover.

[13] It was the custom for Romans to decorate their residences with post-mortem masks of their progenitors, to emphasize how venerable and noble the owner's lineage was.

[14] The symbolic marital bed-chamber, it was separated by a curtain from the atrium.

lord of the manor, the one I had seen in the process of its creation. Racimachos had won: the wart was perched in its place on Caecina's right cheek, the size of a small cherry.

I turned back to the living original. "Don't you want to know what the surprise is?" asked Caecina, eagerly.

I saw that his cheek was now wartless, probably the work of Antonius Muso.[15] The doctor was avaricious, and the income he received from attending to the Emperor's ailments wasn't enough for him. Had Caecina done it to appeal to my mother? Or had she asked him to?

"Fine, don't ask. That's even better, because then I can surprise you too!" He chuckled till his other chin jiggled, but it seemed to me that he was a bit thinner. My mother's doing? Hardly. He had several young female slaves who didn't look as if they worked all that hard doing chores in his extravagant household. But Caecina was in love with my mother, had loved her for the past twenty-five years, feeding his unrequited passion at banquets, and ballooning. Those pretty girls who served us our wine probably did that and nothing more for him.

"All right, but I came to ask you about something else. You told me that Mother had been at the

---

[15] Personal physician to Augustus. It is said of him that he brought the ailing Emperor back from near death a number of times.

Emperor's, and I'm wondering—"

"Wondering what?" asked Caecina quickly. He seemed ill at ease. His cheeks were rather flushed.

"Wondering why she went there," I said. "After all, she isn't actually part of Ovid's immediate family, and as for me, well, as a child I used to call him 'uncle,' but he's an uncle many times removed, if he's an uncle at all. He used to visit us when I was a small child, but he stopped after he married Anicea.[16] He used to bring presents now and then, for me and sometimes for Mother too. Once when he came home from Ilva—"

"You mean that over there?" Caecina pointed to an ebony Venus standing between a marble Leda with the Swan and Minerva in the guise of an African girl, a pigmy at that.

The Venus looked out of place among those solid works of art, I thought.

Caecina apparently read my mind. "She looks out of place there," he sighed. "But Proculeia insisted that—" He fell abruptly silent.

After a while, I said, "Well, that was what I came to ask you. Why? He never so much as wrote her a letter from Pontus."

Now he was truly disconcerted. He started the calisthenics with his interlaced fingers again, the way

---

[16] Ovid's third wife. Her name has been preserved only in the Questus manuscript. A few less than reliable sources give her name as Claudia.

he used to in the old days when he would make calf's eyes at Proculeia and she would offer him her classic profile. I had to giggle. "What's funny?" he asked, blushing. I pointed to his twiddling fingers, and smiled. Caecina quit immediately. We sat in silence. A butterfly flew into the atrium through the *compluvium*.[17]

"So, tell me. What do you think? Why was it?"

"I—" Caecina stopped short again. He turned his little eyes on me in a long, grave look. Just then, I heard an unusual sound for this time of day: wheels rattling outside,[18] and then stopping in front of the house. Caecina took a deep breath, as if he were about to initiate me into some huge mystery, and said, "Questus—"

Just then, Alenus entered the atrium and announced that outside [2 cols] for a bust. As with Caecina, the likeness he had sculpted was a faithful one, but Proculeia defied time. At forty-five, she still looked the same as she had as far back as I could remember, on the litter, when I had sensed rather than registered her beauty, and when all of Rome— all the Rome I knew at that early age—seemed to me

---

[17] A *compluvium* is an opening in the ceiling of the atrium, through which rain would fall into the pool in the centre of the floor (*impluvium*).

[18] An edict by Julius Caesar prohibited the driving of heavy wagons carrying freight in Rome during daylight hours, so they would not impede pedestrians.

as lovely as she was. Now, with the eyes of a grown
man, I looked at the bust Racimachos had made of
her, and indeed, she was like Aphrodite.

But why had she gone to Augustus?

The slaves had carried the bust, still draped with
linen, into the atrium, and there Racimachos had
seized the cloth and dramatically whipped it away.
Since that moment Caecina hadn't uttered a single
articulate sound. Perhaps it was Jupiter who had
ordained that the man's wife should die less than six
months after father did. Now he stood marvelling at
Racimachos's work of art.

Finally regaining his composure, he began eagerly
to bark orders. The slaves lugged the bust to the
tablinum and set it down in front of the curtain and
to the left. On one side stood the immortalized
Caecina, chins, wart, and all, and on the other was
Proculeia, with her wide eyes and splendid Roman
nose. I looked from one to the other and thought of
a line by Ovid's fellow poet, "*Sic visum Veneri ....*"[19]

Sunlight from the *compluvium* illuminated
Proculeia's marble countenance, and a moment later
the real thing, my mother in the flesh, came through
the door. Caecina hurried to greet her, tongue-tied all

---

[19] This is a quotation from Horace's collection *Carmina*
(1.33.10): "*Sic visum Veneri, cui placet impares / Formas atque
animos sub iuga aenea / Saevo mittere cum ioco*" (Such is the
decree of Venus, who decides in cruel jest / to join unequal
minds and bodies / under her yoke of bronze).

over again. Had she married him for my sake? So he would adopt me? After all, she could have

7

Vestalis[20] read while I sipped some Falernian wine and watched him in silence. Making a face, he said, "Do you know how wide the Danube is there? It would take a whole poolful of blood at least!"

Agricola gave a hoarse chuckle at this witticism. Vestalis handed the scroll back to me and tasted the wine, which wasn't bad at all.

"So is he exaggerating? Are you saying it wasn't much of a battle?" I asked.

"The only accurate thing in that poem is the shininess of my armor. I make a point of keeping it

---

[20] Son of the native ("Alpine") prince M. Julius Cottius, of a celebrated and distinguished family. It appears that he did his one-year stint in the military as a senior centurion (*primus pilus*) on the Rhine, under one of Germanicus's legates, and (apparently in A.D. 13) was named legate or prefect (*praefectus orae maritimae*) in charge of the Pontus coast (the Black Sea's shore). Ovid could have been currying his favour because, as a successful soldier and the son of a Roman client king, his intercession with Augustus might be helpful. He apparently overdid his description of the warrior's heroism, as we can see from the fragment. In Book 4.7, he depicts a skirmish as a huge battle, with rivers of blood turning the waters of the Danube scarlet, and the "mountains of corpses" on the battlefield ostensibly slain singlehandedly by Vestalis.

that way, and insist that my men's armor gleam the same way. It usually frightens the barbarians. At Aegisos, they were so intimidated that we only had one casualty: Tarnus, from the first cohort, sprained his ankle jumping down from the fortress wall." He paused. "Could he have described the scene just from reading about it? You were in several battles, did you—"

"Only one," I interjected.

"—did *you* see mountains of corpses?"

"I suffered an accident at the very beginning. But quite a few men did fall there."

"But according to him, the mountains of corpses were supposed to be my doing alone," said Vestalis. Agricola heh-hehed appreciatively again. "Give it here."

I handed Vestalis the scroll. He found what he was looking for and quoted, "'*Mountains of corpses that fell to your blade.*'" He passed the scroll back to me. "As if I were Perseus![21] And I didn't even need the head of Medusa. He makes me—he makes me—" he searched for a metaphor, and finally exclaimed, "Plautus![22] It is as if I had jumped straight out of Plautus!"

---

[21] The context is not entirely clear. Perseus, son of Jupiter, beheaded the Gorgon Medusa and avenged his mother's honor by turning King Polydectes into stone with the monster's head. There may be a connection between his deeds and the implausible account of the military accomplishments of Vestalis.

[22] A Roman dramatist of the day, whose best-known comedy is entitled *The Braggart* (*Miles Gloriosus*), its hero a boastful veteran who grew wealthy from wartime booty.

Just then, a gang of rowdies burst into the tavern and took over a table, all talking and shouting at the same time. Obviously, this wasn't the first place they had stopped to tipple.

"He is a relative of yours, right?" asked Vestalis.

"An uncle of sorts. A very distant relative."

"Then tell him to write about heroes who deserve this kind of praise! Aeschylus, Hercules, Aeneas. Though he'll never outdo Virgil. Tell him to leave me out. Once they've read this in the Fulminata[23] I'll never hear the last of it—they're forever quoting him at dice games as it is. Arguing about who she was. Most of them think it was Julia."

"Then Ovid isn't the only one spreading those tales. So why has the Emperor singled him out to get angry at?" Agricola wondered.

"You're asking the wrong man." Vestalis turned to me. "Please, just write him and ask if this *batrachomyomachia*[24] is intended to make me commit suicide with my own sword. Why has he done this to me? I never did him any harm!"

The poet had Vestalis all wrong. He was a fine fellow, the son of an Alpine prince, but he lived the same rough life as his legionaries. That life was a complete mystery to Ovid, who had never experienced

---

[23] The Fulminata was one of Rome's best-known legions; Vestalis was apparently a familiar figure in its ranks.

[24] An allusion to a Greek parody of the Iliad, recounting a war between frogs and mice in the style of the Homeric epic.

anything remotely like it. Vestalis wasn't like the
egotistic characters who made up Messala's circle of
poets, who would have been flattered by that sort of
poetic hyperbole. Ovid must be desperate

8

that she had taken leave of her senses. They said she
had stopped eating and just sat staring into space
and mumbling to herself. I was not surprised. Marcus
Vesanius[25] was like a cockroach. He wouldn't let up,
even when he was shamed by the poem written

9

which is also why Celsus[26] wanted to go to Tomis."
Cotta[27] wiped the sweat off his forehead. "He
describes Pontus as the Styx and Tomis as Hades.[28]

---

[25] Marcus Vesanius was apparently the model for the unprincipled
hero of Ovid's poem *Ibis*, whose identity has remained a mystery
in other sources.

[26] Probably Albinovanus Celsus, literary protégé of Cottus
Maximus, secretary and comrade to Tiberius, accused by Horace
of literary plagiarism. Nothing more is known of him.

[27] Cotta Maximus was Ovid's friend and patron. He had been
entertaining Ovid at his estate on the island of Ilva (Elba) when
Augustus's decree of *relegatio* against Ovid was delivered there.
According to Ovid, he dissuaded the poet from committing suicide.

[28] In Greek mythology, the Styx is the river across which the
ferryman Charon transports souls to Hades, the underworld, a
gloomy land of the dead.

Flaccus says it's a perfectly pleasant little Getic town, though there are problems in winter with barbarians from the steppes. Nothing serious. The riders from the steppes have never actually overrun the town. Flaccus says it's something like Baiae."

"Exactly," said Curtius. "Flaccus told me it's wonderful[29] in summer. Ovid never writes about Tomis in summer."

"Right. According to him, it's always winter in Tomis. Maybe it's poetic licence, but there's something funny going on. They award him a laurel wreath,[30] but from what he writes, they're exactly like Virgil's Rutulians: living by plunder and corruption and always spoiling for a fight, working the fields wearing gladiators' helmets, and so forth.[31] And have you ever heard of a barbarian using a

---

[29] L. Pomponius Flaccus, a famous soldier, drinking buddy to Tiberius and his comrade in sexual escapades. He apparently interceded with Tiberius on Ovid's behalf (Scr. 3, Frg. 13 and Scr. 4, Frg. 3 and Frg. 5).

[30] Although Ovid was not happy in Tomis, and at the outset he disliked its citizens, they finally recognized him with laurels when he allegedly wrote a poem in praise of the dead Augustus in the Getic language. Some scholars maintain that it was written rather in the pidgin Greek also spoken in Tomis at the time.

[31] The Rutulians were a barbarian tribe, portrayed by Virgil in *The Aeneid* as wild men, living mainly by thievery, who wear helmets even when working in the fields.

quiver? Only in Homer!"[32]

"Is that poetic licence too?" smiled Fabius. "Clinging to the classics and ignoring the grubby present?"

I stopped listening to them. I'd been in the steam room long enough. I got up, left the *laconicum*, and jumped into the cold pool.[33] I was getting tired of hearing them going on and on, belittling Ovid's sufferings. True, he took no interest in the pleasures the town undoubtedly had to offer in the summertime, but they could not understand how his longing for Rome tormented him. His exile inflicted as much misery on his spirit as the bitter cold of Tomis winters. And if he exaggerated the cold of those winters, what of it? When the spirit is in pain, so is the body. Tomis was his Ultima Thule.[34] If his

---

[32] Ovid's word for a bowman's quiver is the Greek *korytos*, which Virgil borrowed in his *Aeneid*. Brutus is trying to prove that Ovid's description of the climate and customs in Tomis is not only grossly exaggerated, it's also based on the classics of Greek and Roman literature, not reality. In other words, he doesn't think Ovid has ever been there.

[33] The cold pool was called the *schola labri*, part of the *caldarium*, a room filled with heated air. In many ways, Roman baths resembled a sauna.

[34] Thule was an island discovered in the distant north by the Greek explorer Pytheas in the fourth century B.C. Its location is unclear, but in Virgil it is seen as a fairytale land somewhere at the very ends of the earth.

yearning for home had not been so fierce, he would have taken it all with humor, would have laughed at his own predicament as easily as his so-called friends here were doing. I decided that what Celsus had failed to do was

10

Yes, I mean Tiberius," said Caecina. "The governor is an old drinking buddy of his. The soldiers call Tiberius 'Biberius Calidus Mero.'[35] But you knew that, didn't you?"

"No," I replied, "I never heard that, not even in the army."

"I have it from my cousin. Aulus was a legate in Moesia[36] when Breucian Bato[37] started acting up in Dalmatia. I know Flaccus, and that nickname would fit him just as well. That is, if his name could be

---

[35] Implies a drunkard; a Latin pun on Tiberius's full name, Tiberius Claudius Nero (*bibo*, "drink"; *calidum*, "hot wine," wine mixed with hot water).

[36] Moesia was a territory south of the Danube, from the Adriatic to the Black Sea.

[37] Breucian Bato was chief of the Breucian tribes in Pannonia, one of Rome's most important provinces, located along the Danube north of Moesia. He was initially an ally to the other Bato mentioned earlier, chief of the Dalmatians and commander of the troops defeated by the Roman legions in the Battle of Andetrium Fortress, where Questus was wounded. He ultimately had Breucian Bato murdered.

punned upon as neatly. Not by me, though, that isn't
something I know how to do. But what I do know is
that Lucius has spent many a night with the
Emperor, paying homage to Bacchus.[38] And not only
to Bacchus. Venus[39] too, and sometimes amusements
with boys."

"But why did Proculeia go to him?" I asked. "And
why did she go to Augustus?"

Crestfallen, Caecina slumped down in his chair.
He glanced at father's death mask on the wall and
sighed. "She went to both of them for the same
reason. But her chances were better with Tiberius.
I'm on good terms with Flaccus, though not the
same way as Tiberius. Flaccus is a splendid fellow.
And Ovid likes him too. You know that he dedicated
several of his epistles from Pontus to him. If anyone
could change the Emperor's mind, it would be
Flaccus."

He was probably right. We sat there in silence,
and Aeria came up softly to refill our wine cups. In
the few years that Caecina had been married to my
mother, we had grown quite close. He no longer
struck me as ludicrous, and I began to take his
liaison with Proculeia seriously. He was wretched as
a senator, more concerned with his own enterprises

---

[38] The Roman god of wine, son of Jupiter.

[39] The Roman goddess of love. Originally the goddess of the
Italian tribes, she gradually took on the attributes of the Greek
Aphrodite.

than with the public good, but in that he was no different from many others. I hadn't known the Senate as it was before Caesar[40] but this was the way it was now and Caecina was more the rule than the exception. Only a few conservative aristocrats still dreamed of the old glory. Caecina extolled the glory of the new Rome. He contributed to it with his marble.

The evening sunlight fell on the marble copy of the *Discus Thrower* that he had given me when I came home from the army. Yes, with his marble, Rome was transformed into a gleaming white city of temples, colonnades, and baths.

"But why?" My question was formal, aimed at getting Caecina to confirm the truth that I had long since guessed. He turned red, making me sorry I had to put him through this.

"You know, lad, Proculeia is very fond of him. At one time, she—" he halted, then he seemed to gather all his courage to say it. "She loved him. But I feel no jealousy for her past, Questus. I have loved her for so many years already, and now, when she—" He stopped as Aeria approached, and when she had refilled our cups again, she left like a wisp of smoke.

---

[40] In the Republic, the Senate represented the supreme power. When Caesar became dictator, he degraded its power considerably. While it formally remained the main authority in the Empire, it had in fact become nothing but a prestige assembly of the Emperor's sycophants.

"You know, Questus, I am not eighteen any more. And Proculeia is far from being a girl herself. Love at our age

II

(when I) peeked into my parents' bedroom. At the same time, there were feelings of tenderness and joy, as if I had known Proculeia when I, no, when *she* was seventeen, as if her loveliness gave her the right to treat me like dirt, and I would still be grateful for a chance to clean off her sandals.

I lay on a couch, alone in the atrium. The *impluvium* was already reflecting Aurora. I had long since sent everyone to bed. This was how Oedipus must have felt, except that he didn't know. I knew. No, it was something else. I had glimpsed Proculeia's lovely mercurial youth, before her beauty had reached the perfection that I myself had seen. Racimachos immortalized it, but—I recalled the line from his colleague's trite poem, "*I have built a monument ....*"[41]

But he ... I raised the book to my eyes and, in Aurora's faint light, I read, "*Could my poems have made her a public figure? That's it: she was prostituted*

---

[41] The reference is, of course, to the famous poem by Ovid's contemporary Horace (Quintus Horatius Flaccus), in which he foretells the immortality of his works. The poem contains the line "*Non omnis moriar*" ("Not all of me will die"), which Ovid paraphrases in his *Black Sea Letters* (*Epistulae ex Ponto*).

by my art ...."[42] I recalled the line "*In one short night ...*"[43] and then the memory of Baiae arose, of Quintus licking his lips as he listened to me reading aloud. Of course, I had no idea then that the mistress I was reading about, who could inspire a man to such Olympic records, was my own mother. I read the lines again: "*I've pimped her charms, I've marked up the route for lovers ....*" I felt as if I were walking the route he had indicated and in Aurora's light it dawned on me that someday the only thing left of Proculeia would be those lines of poetry. Time and the elements would turn Racimachos's exquisite sculpture to dust. Some stranger would buy Caecina's house, other sculptures would grace the atrium, Proculeia's bust would wind up in the garden, wars would roll through Rome, a Hannibal[44] wouldn't stop at the gates of the city, some soldier would carry it off to Africa, or Persia, or Britain, the boat would sink and the statue would come to rest in the mire at the bottom of the sea. I sighed. "*Pimped her charms ....*" Horace, Propertius, Tibullus, Catullus,[45] thanks be to the gods that Rome has

---

[42] *Amores*, Book 3.12, lines 7–8.

[43] See Scr. 1, Frg. 10.

[44] Celebrated Carthaginian general. He missed his chance to wipe out Roman power when, after marching on Rome, he halted before the gates because Carthage failed to send the reinforcements he needed.

[45] All Roman poets, Ovid's contemporaries. All wrote poems about their mistresses.

such pimps. I put down the scroll, set aside my erotic thoughts about the young Proculeia, even though I never considered them sinful. He had transmuted her into poetry: an innocent prostitute who offered herself to one and all.

I turned my thoughts instead to the calendar. When I was born, father had already been home for a year. Before that, he had been on a mission in Egypt for almost two years, where he was delayed by illness and perhaps some other secret imperial mission. After all, he and the Emperor had been friends since the bad times of the Civil War. Then he came home, and I was born that year. But when he lay ill in Egypt, Proculeia had suddenly made up her mind to visit him. She often told me the story of it; such tales always excited me when I was a boy. Their ship had been attacked by pirates, and although it got away, it was so ravaged that it never reached Egypt and barely lurched back to Ostia.

I raised the scroll to my eyes again. It was morning, I could see the words clearly now. I read my father's *propemptikon*.[46] And the next poem but one, the pregnant Corinna,[47] the hasty attempt to abort, her brush with death. Was that hurried trip made to legitimize my older brother? Or my older sister?

---

[46] A poem dedicated to a person setting out on a journey, generally a sea voyage.

[47] Poems 13 and 14 in Book 2 of *Amores* tell of this pregnancy and the abortion that terminated it.

Father survived his illness and returned home, took his place in the Senate and prepared for his new appointment. Before his turn came and he left for Pannonia with Marcus Agrippa,[48] Proculeia had a child. Everything was in order. Everything, thanks to the pirates. Now I knew who I was. And I decided

12

and an opening here. The trick is that when the valve slides under it here, it draws [3 ls] Agricola just shook his head. "How did you ever think of that, Questus?"

"How?" I put down the piece and watched a cargo ship breeze by, bound for Ostia, sails taut with the wind behind them, so that the oarsmen had nothing to do. In my mind's eye, I recalled the rolling Dalmatian countryside, the four glittering ranks, skirmishers streaming back between the maniples of *hastati* and *principes* and the *hastati* advancing to join in one solid, silvery rank, like a machine.

---

[48] Marcus Vispanius Agrippa, leading military personage in the Civil War, devoted friend and ally to Augustus. From general of the legions he was made admiral, and played a decisive role in defeating Marc Antony in the naval battle at Actium. Agrippa invented the *harpax*, significant in that victory. It was a special harpoon, shot from a catapult on the ship's deck to lodge in the beam of the enemy's ship, so it could be pulled in by the Roman sailors, its oars smashed, its crew overpowered by the elite Roman marines.

"Well, whatever, it's a brilliant idea, Questus. But the valve will have to be forged like a sword, tempered and [5 ls] I stared after the departing ship. The oarsmen were rowing lazily. A wave of gloom came over me but once again I observed the power of the oars, and the way

13

but I failed. The Emperor promised Flaccus he would reconsider. But meanwhile, he isn't well, Questus. I heard about it from Anicea. Poor girl, she has completely lost her senses. She can barely walk and now she is going around raving that she is going to follow him to Tomis. And that awful Marcus Vesanius! Ever since he was named legate

SCROLL IV

FRAGMENT

1

landed at Delos[1] on the *ides* of March, replenished
our water and food, and after resting two days we
continued toward Dardanus.[2] The weather was fair,
so we

2

The sun was burning as brightly as it did in Baiae at
this time of year. The sea called Pontus spread blue
and smooth before us, level as a marble floor. Tiny
waves of the incoming tide swished onto the white,
sandy beach. A tiny island appeared in the blue
distance.

I turned to Kalimachos. "Here?" I asked.

"In good weather, he always used to row out there.
He said writing came easily to him on the island."

"He never mentioned that in his letters from
Pontus," I said. I was doubtful about how much of
my Greek Kalimachos comprehended, and his
response confirmed my fears.

"He would usually set out in the morning with the

---

[1] Delos is an island in the Aegean Sea.

[2] Today's Dardanelles.

fishermen, and return before noon. Alone."

I glanced at Agricola. The smith asked, "In this kind of weather?"

Suddenly flustered, Kalimachos replied, "There was a strong wind. Almost a storm. Not even the fishermen—" he stopped short, obviously realizing that he couldn't maintain that Ovid was undeterred by the storm. Besides, on that very day—the day he had represented to us as the fateful one—our ship had been just a few miles out of Tomis and there had been no bad weather.

I asked, "Have you sent word to Rome?"

"We are waiting for an appropriate ship. Will yours be sailing back?"

"I'm not sure." I turned around and looked back at Tomis. A pleasant little town, Flaccus had said. So it appeared. Small houses of white stone, an imitation Greek temple on the hilltop, all surrounded by fortifications. But Ovid had never mentioned that it was on an angled peninsula. "No," I said. "I haven't decided. I hear Poppaeus Sabinus[3] is in Vindobona,[4] or in that new camp, Carnuntum[5]

---

[3] Throughout the reign of Tiberius, Poppaeus Sabinus was a loyal governor in Moesia and Macedonia.

[4] Today's Vienna. An important Roman city, the seat of the Tenth Gemina Legion and the main port for Rome's river fleet.

[5] Originally a permanent military camp on the south bank of the Danube, opposite today's Bratislava (Slovakia), founded under Tiberius. In time it became an important commercial and cultural centre.

3

that if he had decided to take his own life, he would have done it like a Roman.[6] Flaccus had been the legate to Moesia until just recently. Proculeia spoke with him in Rome. He was friendly with Tiberius, and his replacement, his friend Poppaeus, was also a man Tiberius was said to respect. And by repute, an avid reader of poetry.

Agricola interrupted my thoughts. "That fellow is lying." He spoke with the total conviction of an old soldier who doesn't deal in improbabilities.

"What makes you think so? And what about?"

"It's obvious," said the smith, knocking back a slug of wine and scowling. It was an excellent vintage; I don't think I ever had better, not even back in Rome. Nor had Ovid, but the wine was not what kept him in Tomis. Agricola took another swig. "According to you, they didn't like what he wrote about them.[7] So they got rid of him. Hired a killer. Made him disappear."

Why would the people of Tomis kill him? They could easily guess that such a deed wouldn't escape the attention of Rome. For that matter, our Greek guide didn't seem like a fool either, although he couldn't keep his story straight. And as for Augustus, he was no fool; he read poetry, and he must have understood the allusions Ovid had hidden between

---

[6] The Roman way was by slashing the arteries in a bath.

[7] See Scr. III, Frg. 9.

the lines. Yet even in a rage he would not have ordered the poet's murder. Ovid was only sent into exile, and remained a citizen of Rome.

Agricola watched me from behind the Vulcanesque beard he had started growing when he left the army. "He probably annoyed them," he said. "That Greek will tell us some fairy tale to convince us that he drowned. But before that he was going on about how Ovid couldn't get enough of swimming in the sea, and afterwards always lay naked on the beach in the sun." The smith dug into a bowl of polenta that a slave had just brought to our table. "Yes, and then there's the storm they were supposed to have had in Tomis. A small, local storm, right? Localized only in Tomis?" He gave me a eloquent wink.

I shrugged. "I'm not entirely convinced. It's easy to see that Kalimachos is lying. But Tomis honoured him with a laurel wreath. He took the trouble to compose an ode to the Emperor in their Getic tongue—no, my friend, there's more to it than that."

4

the *calends* of July. As our ship approached we saw a brand-new camp spread out before us, built precisely according to regulations. We landed. Agricola and I were both wearing full armor. The letter Flaccus had written opened the gates for us. The legate's palace was still under construction, but the massive main building and the tribunes' houses were finished. In the distance we could see the hospital. The Fourth Flavia Legion was lined up on the training field; a man in a gold-embroidered toga[8] stood facing the ranks of legionaries, haranguing them about something. We were too far away to hear him, but he must have been the legate.

5

only the ground floor of the legate's palace was completed, and Poppaeus had made himself at home there. The *primus pilus* on sentry duty pored over my letter from Flaccus, and that document—invaluable in all of Moesia and the adjoining regions—worked its magic; the pilus waved me in. I climbed the three steps to the archway, and passed between two legionaries. At the end of the corridor, the guard at the doorway to the legate's hall greeted me with a deferential "Lucius Poppaeus is expecting you, Questus Firmus!" I walked in under the Fourth Legion's frowning eagle carved into the doorframe, and through the curtain that hung in the entryway. The illustrious warrior had changed out of the gold-embellished toga, and now was tipping to his lips a gold chalice unlike the work of any Roman craftsman. As I entered, he was reading from an open scroll on the table before him. He placed the chalice beside the scroll and turned to me pleasantly, indicating the chair to the left of the table.

---

[8] The *toga picta* was a ceremonial toga, embroidered with gold thread, that was worn only on festive occasions.

"It is so good to meet you, Questus. Your father and I were on Octavian's staff together, as he no doubt told you." He hadn't, but I nodded, realizing once again how little I knew about Gaius Firmus Siculus. A slave poured wine for me, and Poppaeus leaned back easily in his chair. "I was saddened by his death." He paused. "You have finished your army service?"

"Yes," I replied, and tasted the wine. It was passable, but not as good as the one Kalimachos offered us in Tomis. He had also, very generously, given us a supply to take with us on the long trip along the Danube.

"What brings you to Carnuntum?" Poppaeus watched me with the eyes of an intelligent but also very shrewd commander.

I took my time answering. "My mother asked me to stop here ... to visit a friend. She discussed the matter with your friend Pomponius Flaccus."

Poppaeus nodded, but said nothing.

"The truth is, she did not send me here, to Carnuntum, but to Tomis. Reports that Ovid was in ill health had found their way to Rome. As you know, my mother is his cousin."

Poppaeus raised his eyebrows. "I didn't know that."

"A rather distant cousin, true, but my mother was always fond of him. He often visited us, and his wife, Anicea, is a close friend of my mother's. She would have liked to come to Tomis herself, but her condition is such that it was out of the question."

It seemed to me that a faint smirk crossed his lips. I wondered how much he really knew about all this. He said, "That speaks well of you, Questus. Making so difficult a journey."

"Like almost everyone, Poppaeus, I am an admirer of Ovid's poetry. I wanted to see him again after so many years, before—" I left the sentence hanging, not sure why. "As a boy, I loved him. And now that my mother has taken up his cause—"

"Indeed, Flaccus did speak to me about the matter. The Emperor was inclined to yield, but as you discovered in Tomis—"

He did not finish. I waited a while, but apparently he had thought better of telling me what I might have discovered in Tomis. Finally, I said, "Yes. I discovered that the whole affair stinks."

His glance at me was clearly one of appraisal. "You think so? Why?"

I paused again, and then said, "At the time when Ovid is supposed to have drowned in a storm, my ship was less than half a day's sail from Tomis, and there was no sign of any storm. The weather was perfect."

"I'm no sailor," said Poppaeus, "but I understand that such things happen."

"My captain Heratus says not."

Poppaeus laughed and held out his cup for the slave to refill. I could tell that he had done that more than once today. Much more. "Drink up," he urged me, and tossed off the entire cupful. I did the same, hoping that wine would give me the courage to ask my question. But it didn't. The slave refilled my cup.

"However it happened, Questus, the fact is that Ovid has disappeared."

"Agricola—my friend from our army days—is convinced that the citizens of Tomis murdered him."

"Does he have any proof?"

I shrugged. "I told you the circumstances. He simply drew his own conclusions."

"Hmm," said Poppaeus, thoughtfully. He picked up the scroll and for a long moment there was silence as he rolled back a few pages. "If you are a devotee of Ovid, you will know these lines. Listen to them in the context of what they told you in Tomis." He read: "*I have lost all: only bare life remains to quicken the awareness and substance of my pain. What pleasure do you get from stabbing this dead body? There is no space in me now for another wound.*"[9]

Of course I recognized the passage. It is from a poem in which he says good-bye to his friends, naming them all. It was the kind of letter a person bent on suicide might write. But Ovid's was no suicide note; it was a dramatic verse, a fiction. To think otherwise was nonsense. A wave of grief for the poet came over me.

"Then why," I was fixing Poppaeus with an intent stare, "would the Tomitans invent another scenario?"

---

[9] The closing lines of Book 4.16 of *Black Sea Letters* (*Epistulae ex Ponto*).

"Maybe your friend Agricola is right," said the legate.

"Then you will have to investigate, Poppaeus. Ovid was a citizen of Rome."

Poppaeus nodded. "Then I shall investigate."

I have a feeling for the subtleties a voice can convey. The legate had spoken abruptly, dismissively. He would not have said it that way if he had actually meant it. What did he know? The wine was beginning to have an effect. My courage arrived, and I boldly asked, "How could you have heard about his death? Ours is the first ship to arrive in Carnuntum since it happened."

He was unfazed. "The army receives information through a number of channels," he said. "But I will look into it. I'm sure you will want to wait for the outcome." He stood up to indicate that he was not prepared to give me any more of his time. I rose too, and turned on my heel a little unsteadily. We had said our farewells and I was almost through the doorway when he called after me, "But do visit Vindobona. They're giving a new *trabeata*[10] in the theatre there, by some pupil of Melissus, Pomponius Pinnatus. I'm told it's very funny. And enlightening too."

---

[10] Social comedy from the milieu of the Roman *equites*. It was developed by Gaius Cilnius Melissus, one of the protégés of Maecenas, famous patron of the arts whose name has come, in many languages, to symbolize a wealthy person who supports artists.

I stopped short. What did he mean by that? "I've never heard of him. Pinnatus?"

"Yes. He's a veteran, very well read. He's produced the play with a cast of legionaries and officers' wives. Also some wives of local merchants."

I was amazed. "No professional actors?"

"None at all," said Poppaeus. "It's a novelty, of course. In Rome, it probably couldn't be done. Nor would it be necessary, though. Of course, this *municipium* is no Rome."

"A veteran? And a pupil of Melissus?"

"After his release from service, he spent time in Rome."

"I never heard of him there. And why is he here, when—?"

"He was with the Tenth Gemina," Poppaeus interrupted. He was beginning to sound testy, pacing around the table. It was high time I left. "Maybe he wanted to try out the piece here, before daring to bring it to Rome. There are about three more performances. It was a great success. The author attends every performance. I think he'll be pleased to meet you. Good-bye."

I walked out into the hall, trying not to show how shaky I was. Why, after all that, had he recommended— and so insistently—that I go to see some comedy? I wasn't in the mood for some twittering patrician farce. Was I imagining it, or was he trying to tell me something with his odd remarks?

I wondered: could the answer be in the Vindobona theatre? But this was all nonsense. I turned my steps toward the hospital, where

6

the sounds of *bucinae*.[11] Those patrons who were
still mobile—including me—staggered out of the
tavern. A legion was marching past. In the lead,
directly behind the eagle, came the *bucina* players,
followed by their legate on horseback. I recognized
him: Lucius Donatus Africanus. Behind him came
the banners, and ranks of legionaries in gleaming
armour; it was a magnificent procession. The patrons
of the tavern could hardly believe their eyes. I looked
around and suddenly stopped in my tracks. Marcus
Vesanius? In Vindobona? Yes, it was. He was sitting
in a litter on the corner, waiting for the parade to
pass, staring listlessly

7

(hung) a handbill advertising the comedy *The
Faithful Husband* by that author I had never heard
of. People were beginning to drift into the theatre. I
followed them. My senatorial toga got me a seat in
the second row. Agricola sat down further back. The
front row was full; the legate sat in the middle,
surrounded by his staff and officers' wives. At the
end of the row sat another annoying surprise, in a
senatorial toga, alone. What was *he* doing here? I
hoped he hadn't seen me. Turning my head away, I
rested my elbow on my knee and my chin in my hand,
as if I were deep in thought. Just then

---

[11] Brass musical instruments blown on ceremonial occasions.

8

was here for the beginning. Let me see if I can find
him." He looked around the roomful of "actors,"
gestured to me to stay where I was and ran out into
the hall. Suddenly a woman's screech sounded from
there.

Galbus returned. "He must have left during the
performance," he said, perturbed. "He was here
yesterday too, sat here through the entire play and
afterwards even joined us at the tavern." He took
another look around. "Maybe he felt sick. He was
drinking pretty heavily all evening."

I knew that wasn't why he left. No, he had also
recognized the person I saw in the audience, and
clearly that was reason enough for him to bolt. But
where? I had to

9

Furnilla,[12] and her husband's name is Gaius
Invalidus Sicanus.[13] But everybody knows who it's
really about. And the author has his characters
talking openly about why Capito[14] was obliged to
leave Rome!"

"The fool!" said Poppaeus peevishly. He cursed

---

[12] Undoubtedly the Empress Livia.

[13] A character in Ovid's comedy, apparently representing
Augustus himself, all his life in fragile health.

[14] A man with a big head. In the comedy, clearly Ovid himself,
whose *cognomen* Naso was derived from *nasus*, "nose."

and started pacing back and forth. Then he stopped and turned to me. "I investigated, understand? Ovid was drowned in a storm and his body was never found. Understand?" I understood all too well. He resumed his pacing. "I have to do something about him, but what?"

Indeed. Where could the poor wretch go? Grief overcame me as I thought of my father's anguish.

"Wait a moment," said the legate pensively. "It may be a crazy notion, but ... I'll give you a letter and we'll

SCROLL V

This scroll is severely damaged, with only three fragments remaining legible. The last one is apparently a section of the play The Faithful Husband.

FRAGMENT

I

hurried back to Rome, Mother, to forestall your grief. At least you know he isn't dead."

"He might as well be," said Proculeia, wearily. "Marcus Vesanius saw the play!" My mother's slender hand rested on the scroll with my father's comedy, which I had brought her from Carnuntum. Her fingers closed tightly around it. "He is dead," she whispered.

"It may be possible to arrange it somehow," said Caecina uncertainly. "After all, Tiberius did agree. And in Rome today, anything can—" He stopped. The thought was unthinkable. "The garrisons in Pannonia cost a lot of money," he said, and fell silent again. He turned his little eyes to Proculeia, and then to me. Because neither of us said a word, he continued nervously, "Marcus Vesanius tells tales through Livia. Tiberius can't stand him. And Livia— even if she is his mother, she—"[1]

"It'll kill him, I know it will. He was dying a slow death of heartache in Tomis, but this is too much. This is really a death sentence."

"Does anyone know about it?" asked Caecina.

"Only Poppaeus," I replied. "He gave me the letter for Cunobelinus. And Agricola, of course. He's the one who asked around and found the merchant. I paid the man, but didn't wait around to see what happened. I decided it would be best if I returned to Rome. Poppaeus also gave me a letter for Tiberius. I hoped I could get here before someone from Tomis came and told you he drowned."

"Will you approach Tiberius?" Proculeia anxiously turned to her husband.

"I will. I already have an appointment to see him," said Caecina.

2

on the steps to the Temple of Divus Julius.[2] It was a lovely Roman autumn day. Caecina's marble gleamed all around me, and reminded me of the beach in Tomis, its white sand bright in the sunlight beside

---

[1] Caecina is alluding to Tiberius's hatred of Livia, which was common knowledge.

[2] The Temple of Divus Julius was a shrine consecrated to the memory of Julius Caesar in Rome's Forum.

the blue water, where Ovid was declared to have drowned. And by decision of the legate at Carnuntum, he is now officially dead.

In the Forum the usual clusters of senators and their clients, rich merchants—as rich as Caecina— were gathered and youths in brand-new togas of manhood were strutting around with their prettied-up girls. I sat there with the unhappy Caecina. This was Ovid's world; he belonged here, but had been driven out by the antagonism of a woman—the murderous Empress. He had evened the score, though, with his comedy.

Caecina sighed. "We fared as badly as the legions at Teutoburg Forest.[3] Good thing you had that letter."

I laid a hand on his shoulder. Life is a strange play. And it doesn't follow Aristotle's rules, either.[4] The pudgy merchant of marble used to seem foolish to me, but now I loved him, for his loyalty. "Right, Caecina. Good thing I had the letter."

Curtius Atticus was striding across the Forum like a man in his cups, ramming people as he went. He

---

[3] The Teutoburg Forest was the site of the battle in A.D. 9, in which the Cheruscan leader Arminius wiped out three legions of Quinctilius Varus. It was the worst defeat of Roman troops during the life of Augustus, and almost drove the Emperor to despair.

[4] Aristotle's *Poetics* outlines the rules of the classic Greek drama, insisting, for example, that the action it represents must last no longer than a single revolution of the sun.

spied us and hastily turned to the temple staircase. A closer look showed the tears flowing down his cheeks. Another loyal

3

	such stamina? Really? Such a constitution!
FURNILLA	Indeed!
CAPITO	You are to be congratulated.
FURNILLA	But do you know how tiring it is?
CAPITO	Well, you can't have everything.
PLAUTUS	It is what Lentilla dreams of.
FURNILLA	Who is that?
PLAUTUS	My concubine. I'm not enough for her. What she needs is a man like Gaius Invalidus Sicanus.
CAPITO	Well then, with your permission, Furnilla, and of course, if Gaius is willing.

The foregoing fragment has been transcribed in the manner of contemporary graphic layout for play scripts.

SCROLL VI

*Two fragments are all that remain legible of this scroll,
which was for the most part completely destroyed.*

FRAGMENT

1

along the Tiber. We set sail early in the morning, so
we would not be noticed if—as happened that time
after dinner with (Augustus)

2

then wouldn't the water just fall off it?" Cornelius
Fidus[1] was incredibly ignorant. I never did understand
why my sister married him. Or why her intelligent
father wanted her to marry a dolt. But Venus, of
course, is unpredictable.

---

[1] A senator, husband to Ovid's daughter by his second wife. The
only information about him in the literature is that he burst into
tears in the Senate when General Corbulo derisively referred to
him as a "shabby peacock." His discussion with Questus apparently concerned the hypothetical question of how the oceans of
the world would adhere to the earth if it were really round.

Patiently, I started explaining, "Tell me, Cornelius, what happens when you hurl a javelin?"

He gave me a puzzled look. "I am a senator, Questus

SCROLL VII

FRAGMENT

I

in the fifteenth year of his rule.[1] I prayed to the masks
of Proculeia and Caecina for an auspicious journey.
It was July, day four before the *nones*, just two years
after Proculeia had died[2] and Caecina had committed
suicide in the Roman manner. I had entrusted the
administration of my property—which had multiplied
by virtue of the two legacies I received—to Quintus.
Nothing had ever cast a shadow on our friendship, a
good Roman *sodalicium*. At the time, Quintus was
also very wealthy, but unlike me he had disobeyed his
father, opting for life in the shadows,[3] as Ovid had
done. Unlike Ovid, however, he had devoted himself
to the study of history. In his earlier years, his *History*

---

[1] The fifteenth year of his rule would have been A.D. 29, fifteen
years after Tiberius came to power.

[2] From this it may be inferred that Questus's mother died in A.D.
27, at approximately sixty.

[3] *Vita umbratilis* is a mildly pejorative reference to the situation
of a Roman aristocrat who turned his back on the customary
political or military career and instead took up another career,
especially one in philosophy or poetry.

of Crete brought him considerable fame, and for the past twenty years he has been working on a history of Roman naval battles. From research he had done in that context in libraries in Rome and Alexandria, he had gained a breadth of knowledge about the structure of ships, which was to stand me in good stead. It was Quintus who advised me not to turn my back on the tried and tested type of mercantile *moneris*[4] for [about 3 ls] winds die down. So I hired a party of experienced Greek oarsmen and equipped the ship with a new system of sails that enabled us to maneuvre against the wind. Quintus wanted to go with me. The excitement that was driving me into that wild unknown had infected him too. But I convinced him that he must stay in Rome. I had no one to

2

able to fully replenish our stores of wood and it was the *ides* of November by the time we sailed west. The boy Tesotulus[5] joined our company. His Latin had become quite fluent. Aemilius Regalianus[6] grumbled

---

[4] A ship with a single bank of oars.

[5] As would Columbus fourteen centuries later, Questus apparently landed on an island in the Caribbean. For an interpreter, he would have hired a youth who would quickly pick up Latin. The unknown native names are obviously converted by Questus into Latin forms in the manuscript (e.g., Telalocus, Tesotulus).

[6] Aemilius Regalianus was apparently a linguist whom Questus had recruited for the voyage.

that I wouldn't need him any more, now that I had
an interpreter, but he took it all in stride, and
besides, he was avidly studying with Tesotulus the
language of the lad's island.

A month passed before

3

they had seen smoke rising straight up, as there was
no wind. Soon after sunrise, the entire town had
gathered on the shore, with King Telalocus sitting high
in his litter, surrounded by priests and commanders,
waiting for a volcano to rise from the sea[7]

---

[7] Here we find the sole direct indication that Questus's ship was
steam-driven. Questus apparently landed on the south shore of
the Gulf of Mexico, where the swampy plains around the Laguna
de los Cerros had once been the seat of the mature Olmec
civilization. This culture vanished from the archaeological record
around A.D. 400; the reason for its disappearance is unknown,
but it did lay the groundwork for the civilizations that would
follow. It is regrettable that so little has been preserved of this
particular scroll, but even the little that we have shows people
like King Telalocus as being capable of considerable sophistication.
It is evidence that the culture of the land had evolved, as had
imperial Rome, to a stage characterized by a clash between
official religion and privately held doubts. Telalocus may have
been a king of the transitional period between the remnants of
the Olmec culture and the beginning of the Mayan, which
would blossom in many centres across today's Mexico, Belize,
Guatemala, and Honduras about three hundred years after

4

into a swan?"[8] King Telalocus leaned back and laughed aloud. Even Tesotulus giggled, but immediately put on a serious face, fearful that the king would consider it a sign of disrespect to the gods of his guests. But King Telalocus kept on laughing: "Tetasilan also likes to change into animals, but never for so human a purpose. Your theology is hilarious, Questus. And how about that jealous wife of his!" He was shaking with mirth.

Aemilius and I exchanged glances. This king acted

Questus's landing. Honduras became the site of the grandest of the Mayan cities, although it was on the outer periphery of the Maya's area of influence. That city was Copán, where the seven scrolls of the Questus manuscript were discovered in the structure known as "Rosalia." As for conjectures about how a manuscript written four centuries earlier found its way to Copán, see my introduction on page seven.

[8] Questus had obviously been acquainting Telalocus with Roman and Greek mythology. Jupiter (the Greek Zeus) changed himself into a cob, a male swan, in order to seduce the lovely Leda; his wife Juno (the Greek Hera) made life miserable for the lord of Olympus, his mistresses, and his children. Greco-Roman deities behaved for the most part like mortals, in the best and worst senses. During the time of the Empire, educated Romans still paid formal obeisance to the old gods while privately not giving them much credence. In that sense, King Telalocus "was acting like a Roman."

like a Roman. With us, anyway. When his priests were around, he was solemn

5

on the flat roof of the palace. "You say that is what the earth is like?" asked Telalocus, staring at the full moon reflected in a sea as smooth as a marble floor.

"It is," I said. "In fact, Eratosthenes[9] even measured its circumference." I proceeded to explain to the king the trigonometry that Eratosthenes had used.

---

[9] Eratosthenes was a drama critic and librarian of the great library at Alexandria in the third century B.C. He noticed that on 21 June, the vernal equinox, the sun shone straight down into a well in Syene (today's Aswan). Already believing that the earth is round, he theorized that the rays of the sun must strike different places on the earth at different angles, and cast a measurable shadow accordingly. He assumed Alexandria to be directly to the north of Syene, which gave him two locations on the same meridian of longitude. He took a column of known height and observed the shadow it cast in the sunlight of the summer solstice in Alexandria. Its angle was about one-fiftieth of a circle. Then he multiplied the distance between Syene and Alexandria by 50, and came up with the circumference of the earth as approximately 25,200 of today's miles. The circumference is in fact 24,860 miles, an infinitesimal difference. Eratosthenes' calculation was much more accurate than the one made seventeen centuries later by Columbus, who estimated the earth to be far smaller than—as Questus knew—it actually was, and on that basis sailed off impetuously into the unknown.

Telalocus withdrew into his thoughts. For a long while, we sat in silence. Then he turned to me. "And what does Eratosthenes say to your hilarious theology?"

"I have no idea. I don't think he ever wrote anything about it."

"And you? Do you believe in gods that are so human?" He was full of surprises. He did indeed remind me of a Roman.

"No," I replied. "In Rome, educated people do not believe in them."

"So what do you picture? Something like that?" He indicated the moon.

I shook my head. "No. I believe, like Aristotle[10]

6

but it is so far away. Our boats cannot get (there)[11]

---

[10] Aristotle believed that there was only one god.

[11] This is where the manuscript ends. What happened to Questus after that is a mystery, but it seems certain that he did not return to Rome, "...*but it is so far away. Our boats cannot get there...*," is probably a snatch of dialogue with King Telalocus, and it is possible that Questus set sail for a place that the king's boats were unable to reach. We have no idea where or why, but he probably perished there.

COMMENTARY

BY PATRICK OLIVER ENFIELD

S ince I am by profession a mystery writer, whose job it is to think up solutions to such riddles, my publisher had the crazy idea that I should write the commentary for this Roman mystery.

Two mysteries dominate this fragmentary chronicle. The first is Ovid's destiny after he was sentenced to *relegatio* (a milder form of banishment, with no loss of property, whereas *exilio* entailed the confiscation of the person's goods and possessions) to the town of Tomis, on the shore of what was then known as the Pontus, today the Black Sea. The second is the manner in which the chronicler, Questus Firmus Siculus, came to the American continent. Also connected with the Ovid component of the story is the question of the paternity of the same Questus Firmus Siculus, whose official father was Gaius Firmus Siculus, politician and soldier in the time of Augustus, and finally also the matter of Augustus's true reason for banishing Ovid to exile.

The authenticity of Questus's text has been repeatedly confirmed by laboratory tests (see *Report* on this matter by Professor Quido Hermann Schonberg of Harvard University and Professor

Lorraine Linda Burnside of Yale University) and linguistic analyses. This being the case, it is my position that his account of historical circumstances must be considered authoritative despite being uncorroborated by subsequent histories (e.g., the names of Ovid's wives do not appear in any other documented source) and being occasionally subjective or inexplicable (e.g., the Roman system of battle, which Questus credits with inspiring his invention).

The family of Questus Firmus Siculus does not appear in any historical record. The minuscule Scroll 2, Fragment 1 (hereinafter designated by abbreviations: Scr. 2, Frg. 1) introduces nothing but a *nomen* and *cognomen*, and it is only from context later in the narrative that we realize that it is the name of Questus's father; the man's *praenomen*, Gaius, is disclosed in Scr. 2, Frg. 6.

We do not know exactly when the father was born, but we are told that he was from one of the "oldest and wealthiest (families) in Rome" (Scr. 1, Frg. 7) and that during the Civil War he "had always been [Augustus's] staunch friend and ally" (Scr. 1, Frg. 11). It may be assumed, then, that when Civil War broke out in 49 B.C., Gaius was at least twenty years old, and may have been considerably older, given the evidence that his military career was already flourishing during the war.

We also know when he died (Scr. 2, Frg. 6): it was at the time of the battle for Andetrium fortress at Salonae in A.D. 8, where Questus was wounded. In return for his aforementioned staunch loyalty to

Augustus, Gaius had "accumulated even more
(property)" (Scr. 1, Frg. 7), and the high point of his
career was when Augustus named him his legate
(Scr. 1, Frg. 11), *legatus Augusti pro praetore*, i.e., the
governor of an imperial province (we find no mention
of which one), whose jurisdiction included all the
troops located in the area. This post was evidently
the main source of the spoils that we are told Gaius
Firmus "accumulated." His career apparently
continued after the war (see, for example, Scr. 3,
Frg. 11: the "secret imperial mission" in Egypt). He
obviously did not get along with his son, who refused
to embark on a political career: witness the complaint
he makes against the young Questus after the
Emperor's banquet (Scr. 1, Frg. 11), and in their
exchange in the arena, where the two of them attend
a gladiatorial bout (Scr. 1, Frg. 13).

The date of birth of Questus's mother is also
unknown to us, but it was in all probability shortly
after the naval battle at Actium in 31 B.C., which
ended the Civil War and elevated Octavian to the
imperial throne with the grand title of "Augustus."
My surmise that she was born at about this time is
based on several contexts that will become apparent
further on. Her *praenomen* was Proculeia, her second
name Aemilia and her *cognomen* Saepuli (in Scr. 2,
Frg. 6, her brother has the *cognomen* Saepulus). She
died in A.D. 27, two years before Questus set out
across the sea ("in the fifteenth year of [Tiberius's]
rule," i.e., A.D. 29), for in Scr. 7, Frg. 1, he describes
praying then to her death mask.

Questus undoubtedly adored his mother. Several of the episodes that have remained to us are evidence of that, the most compelling being in Scr. 1, Frg. 6, when the slaves are bearing the litter with Proculeia on the Aventine. Proculeia "wore gold earrings and was always beautiful and fragrant," and it appears to little Questus on her lap that "all of Rome smelled like Mama." This childish perception is also recalled during the feast with Augustus, when as a young man (he had just put on his first *toga virilis*, the toga of manhood) it seems to him "that the entire banquet hall was redolent of her perfume, the fragrance of Rome that I remembered from those days long past when we went on our outings in the litter," and when he says he feels "proud of my mother, Proculeia; she was as lovely as Aphrodite" (Scr. 1, Frg. 11).

Many similar appreciative references to his mother's beauty testify to his intense filial love, and culminate in the scene when he is looking into his parents' bedroom from the atrium (Scr. 3, Frg. 11) in his father's house. By this time, the father is dead and Proculeia has married Caecina and moved with him into his opulent home. There, in the old bedroom, Questus feels that he has had "a glimpse of Proculeia's lovely, mercurial youth, before her beauty had reached the perfection that I myself had witnessed." There he also deduces that Proculeia is Ovid's Corinna and that his father is not Gaius Firmus but Publius Ovidius Naso. For that matter, in the preceding fragment (Scr. 3, Frg. 10) Caecina essentially tells him outright: "You know, lad,

Proculeia is very fond of him. At one time, she ...
she loved him." That also explains Proculeia's visits
to the two emperors, and Caecina's as well: both of
them intercede on behalf of the delinquent poet, in
hopes of obtaining imperial permission for him to
return to Rome, or at least to relocate to one of the
Roman towns near the border, where there would
have been an approximation of the social life of
Rome, with baths, arenas, theatres—in short, conditions far removed from his desolate existence in
Tomis.

One question arises in the context of Questus's
filial (merely filial?) love for his mother, and that is
whether Questus was married. It appears that he was
not, or perhaps that his union was one of duty or
tradition, and hence not worth mentioning in his
narrative. Be that as it may, his marital status and his
silence on the subject were apparently connected to
Augustus's matrimonial laws. *Lex Julia de maritandis
ordinibus* (18 B.C.) was the Emperor's attempt to
stem the decline in the population of Rome. Under
this law, married men with children were rewarded,
while unmarried or divorced men were penalized.
The law evoked considerable opposition, however,
and in A.D. 9 Augustus modified it with *Lex Papia
Poppaea*, which allowed a number of legitimate
reasons for celibacy. It is possible, then, that Questus
took advantage of the benefits afforded by the latter
law and remained a bachelor.

An important role in Questus's story is taken by
Spurius Caecina Ventro, a long-time admirer of

Proculeia. After the death of her husband, Ventro's constancy is rewarded when he at last marries Proculeia. We find no mention of him in historical sources, but we know of the existence of his cousin Aulus (Scr. 3, Frg. 10), legate in Moesia. Aulus Caecina Severus is referred to in historical sources as one of the most capable of Augustus's generals. He made his name in numerous battles, commanded the army in Northern Germania, served as long as forty years, and had six children, although he held the opinion that provincial governors and commanders should not be allowed to take their wives with them into the field, so as not to be distracted from their duties to the Empire.

There is an immense amount of literature about Ovid's banishment from Rome, but the real reason for such a radical measure being taken against an extremely popular poet has never been satisfactorily determined. The main historical sources—the writings of Roman historians detailing the time of the Emperor's edict—have not been preserved. As for Ovid's comedy, in which the author ostensibly reveals the reason (Scr. 4, Frg. 9: "[the characters speak] openly about why Capito was obliged to leave Rome!"), only a negligible snippet can be salvaged from Questus's narrative. It is enough, however, to allow us to conclude that the comedy was close in tone to some scenes in *Amores* and *Ars Amatoria*, the books that so incensed the Emperor. Although the play remains otherwise unknown, it seems probable that it would contradict the commonly held opinion that, in his poems written in Tomis, Ovid was grossly obsequious to Augustus. The error of this widely accepted view is obvious from Questus's report of the discussion among Ovid's friends in Brutus's home (Scr. 3, Frg. 5 and 9). Their references to the content of Ovid's poem make it clear that certain passages can only be understood as sarcasm aimed directly at the Emperor.

Life in a "barbarian" environment would understandably have driven the poet, accustomed to the amenities of civilized Rome, to the brink of desperation, which apparently led him to overstate the hardships of his life in the climate in Tomis. For a Roman, the only real discomfort in the coastal town would have been its winter season, however brief. The long spring and summer there are known to have been more than pleasant. Today, the place that was Tomis is the spa town of Constanza (Constanta), a Romanian seaside tourist centre, where the average winter temperature is 37°F (about 3°C) by day, and 25°F (about minus 4°C) by night; the maximum summer temperature, in July and August, is 79°F by day and 63°F by night (about 28°C and 17°C degrees, respectively).

So Ovid's friends (and some modern scholars as well) may be justified in concluding that Ovid presented Tomis as being worse than it was. In fact, some go so far as to deny that Ovid ever lived there (e.g., A. D. Fitton Brown), hypothesizing that the poet only pretended to leave for Tomis, and actually took refuge with friends. Thus the plaintive poems he addressed to the Emperor, pleading with him to reverse his edict and allow him to "return," were sent from a secret location in Rome itself.

One of the arguments for this theory is raised by Ovid's friends as well (Scr. 3, Frg. 9). Scholars have meticulously compared Ovid's climatic, geographical, and ethnographic references to Tomis and its inhabitants with similar references by older poets (Virgil, Homer), who demonstrably had never been there, and have found marked similarities between Ovid's observations and those of the classics. This is also suggested by the soldier Vestalis, the hero of Letter 7, Book 4 of the *Black Sea Letters* (*Epistulae ex Ponto*), whose military exploits in the minor skirmish at Tomis are described by Ovid in the manner of the heroic battles in Virgil or Homer (Scr. 3, Frg. 7).

Be that as it may, I am convinced that Questus is justified when he dismisses the arguments of his friends who are debating the subject in the baths (Scr. 3, Frg. 9) and concludes that "when the spirit is in pain, so is the body."

But let us return to the experts who surmise that the damning poems were only a pretext for Ovid's *relegatio*, referring to evidence that Augustus himself (at least in his youth) had been a less than shining example of sexual morality. It was only when he became Emperor that he decided to bring Roman morals back to the pristine purity conventionally attributed to the early Republic.

These critics point to the curious fact that Ovid's repudiation came as late as eight years after the

damning poem was initially made public. I believe,
however, that what is often forgotten is that *Ars
amatoria* was a huge public success, something akin
to today's best-sellers. It went through a number of
editions, and literally everyone in Rome was familiar
with it. Proof that it was popular not only with
educated readers is, for example, in the quotations
preserved on the walls of the bordellos of Pompeii.
At the very least, the extraordinary and continuing
popularity of the book (and the author) contributed
to the Emperor's decision. But perhaps the scholars
are right, and the main reason for Ovid's punishment
must be sought elsewhere.

Where, then?

The notion that the poet surprised the Emperor's
wife naked in the bath or the Emperor himself in an
act of pederasty can be relegated to the category of
malicious gossip, too often credited by Latin authors,
even those as significant as Suetonius. Another, more
serious, line of argument suggests that Ovid may
have been involved somehow in the failed conspiracy
against Augustus led by Lucius Aemillius Paullus,
who paid for the attempt with his life on the execution ground. This theory holds that Ovid escaped a
similar fate only by virtue of his fame as a poet.

It strikes me that, rather than dangerous political
machinations, the successful poet and lover of life
(and hence a man hardly disposed to risk his own life
lightly) may have been involved with Julia, granddaughter to Augustus and wife to Paullus. Like her
mother, she was well known for her dissolute way of

life, and after her husband's execution the Emperor
exiled her to the tiny island of Trimerium (or
Trimerus) off the Apulia coast. There she languished
for another twenty years, maintained by a secret
allowance made to her by Augustus's wife, Livia.

As for the sedition theory, records exist that
suggest Ovid lent his lodgings for a meeting of the
conspirators—which would have been sufficient
cause for imperial justice to count him among their
number—but it is also possible (and more likely) that
he inadvertently found himself where they were
meeting, with no idea of what they were planning,
and hence no reason to report the meeting as subver-
sive. (Perhaps that was the familiar "*error*" to which
the poet refers to, together with "a poem"—in the
original Latin, "*carmen*"—in line 207, Book 2 of
Tristia and elsewhere.) Finally, some say that his sole
connection with the conspiracy was that he cuck-
olded its leader Paullus. That does not strike me as
convincing. It seems that once married, Ovid had a
spotless reputation.

One fragment in the Questus text (Scr. 2, Frg. 5)
offers yet another possibility. Lying wounded and
bored in the military hospital in Salonae, Questus
pursues a train of thought. He recalls a bedroom
scene with the slave Cynthia, his first concubine,
and an interesting anecdote she related about a
banquet, evidently in his father's house, at which she
overheard Augustus ask Ovid sarcastically when
he would marry again, and saw the poet turn a
"senatorial purple," whereupon the Emperor asked

Proculeia, with equal sarcasm, how her new baby
was doing. Proculeia "raised her head defiantly," but
before the perceptive Cynthia has time to explain to
Questus why the question so peeved Ovid, footsteps
sound outside the door and the girl flees hastily from
the youth's bed and room.

Did Augustus know that Corinna, the heroine of
Ovid's apparently newly published *Amores*, was in
fact Proculeia? And did he deduce—as Questus
would so many years later—that Aemilia's baby
(himself) was in fact not sired by the imperial
emissary to Egypt?

He may well have known, because he had his own
informers. Moreover, there is yet another relevant
scene in the Questus manuscript, one in the baths at
Baiae (Scr. 1, Frg. 10). There, the narrator's friend
Quintus speculates that Ovid's first wife Racilia had
been unfaithful to the poet with the Emperor, but
that "'he couldn't very well put that in a poem, and
in his latest work, *he* is the one doing the cuckolding.'" Questus asks whether it is the Emperor
he is cuckolding, and "Quintus glanced around
nervously." Unfortunately, there are two illegible
columns at this point in the manuscript, but it can
be assumed from his "nervous" glance around that
Ovid's love was the wife of someone of great
prominence.

Augustus?

If the Emperor had in fact seduced Racilia, Ovid
could not write about it, for obvious reasons. In *Ars
Amatoria*, however, he describes various techniques

for the seduction of married women, which may contain allusions intelligible only to his contemporaries —allusions to the poet's other amatory adventures; other, that is, than the one openly described in the book *Amores*, with a lady intimately celebrated, though, of course, not mentioned by her real name. These concealed hints might refer to an affair that was gossiped about in knowledgeable circles of Roman society, and even, as Quintus says, "in the Forum." A scandalous affair, then, between the poet and whom?

The Empress?

Considering what we know about the marriage between Augustus and Livia, and about Ovid's second and third marriages, it seems highly unlikely. The Emperor married Livia in 38 B.C. following a convoluted course of matrimonial diplomacy difficult for us to grasp in this day and age, and rather provocative even in a Rome accustomed to similar complexities. Nonetheless, historical sources indicate that the union was a happy one and lasted until the death of Augustus in A.D. 14. Livia survived her husband by fifteen years and died, at eighty-six, in A.D. 29.

In about 15 B.C., Ovid married his second wife, but she died soon thereafter, perhaps while giving birth to Ovid's only daughter, or during the birth of another child, which also died. He married for a third time shortly after his father died, in about 1 B.C.; the poet was then forty-five years old. His new wife brought with her a daughter, Perilla, from a previous marriage. The names of Ovid's wives have not been preserved, but we discover in the Questus manuscript that this third wife's name was Anicea (Scr. 3, Frg. 6 and 13). The marriage was apparently a happy one, and when the Emperor exiled Ovid to Tomis, Anicea only remained in Rome to protect the poet's property from the designs of various "interested parties." Topping the list of these parties is the antihero of Ovid's poetic tract *Ibis*. Until now it was assumed that this was a fictitious character, more a convenient embodiment of all the negative attributes of those parties interested in the exiled poet's property. We discover, however, from the Questus manuscript, that it was a specific individual named Marcus Vesanius, legate of a division (we are not told which one).

Now let us do a little arithmetic. Ovid's first marriage falls in the year 27 B.C., lasts less than a year and ends in divorce. At that time, the Emperor, alleged seducer of this one of Ovid's wives, has been living in an exemplary union with Livia for eleven years, and has gained a reputation as a renowned moralizer. So, can we believe that he was guilty of a marital infidelity that until now was successfully concealed?

Theoretically, it is possible. Imperial Rome was not like twenty-first-century America, where any and all sexual indiscretions committed by public figures are inevitably found out and sensationalized in tabloids and even the more respectable media. True, not much escaped the attention of the Forum, but there was no printed press, tabloid or otherwise.

And not only theoretically. It was even possible practically, if we are to believe Octavian's colleague (later his mortal enemy) Antony. In his biography of Augustus, Suetonius quotes Antony's sarcastic comment in a letter to Augustus. Defending himself before the Emperor's moral outrage over his famous relationship with Egyptian Queen Cleopatra, he wrote: "What's come over you? Is it because I go to bed with the queen? Please! It isn't as if it's something new, is it? Haven't I been doing it for nine years now? And what about you, is Livia the only woman you go to bed with? I congratulate you if at the time you read this letter you haven't also had Tertulla or Terentilla or Rufilla or Salvia Titisenia or the whole lot of them. Does it really matter where you get a stand or who the woman is?"

This letter was recorded by Suetonius in his *Lives of the Caesars (De Vita Caesarum)*. He is not an author noted for any particular historical accuracy, but if we are to believe him here (the letter is cited in many works about Augustus), the Emperor— married or single—did not deny himself any sexual pleasures. And Antony is not the only source in this context. If what Questus told Quintus is true, we can assume that Ovid had some sort of unsettled accounts with the Emperor. From the tale told by the slave Cynthia, it would appear that the Emperor was holding Ovid in check by what he knew about the poet's relationship with Proculeia. Did Ovid, then, try to square accounts by seducing the Emperor's wife?

He apparently was audacious enough—after all,

he first published his explicit poems in 15 B.C., that is to say, well after the Emperor had launched his campaign to restore strict morality to society with the issuance of his law *lex Julia de maritandis ordinibus* in 18 B.C. His triumphs as a poet evidently gave Ovid, this playboy of antiquity, a sense not only of being immortal (see *Tristia*, Book 4.10 and elsewhere), but also invulnerable.

What about Livia, though?

History tells us that as a wife she was blameless. True, there are serious suspicions that she committed several murders (in the interest of her son Tiberius, whom she was determined to make successor to Augustus against the designs of various of the Emperor's blood relatives), but historical sources are silent about any sexual adventures she might have had. On the other hand, history makes no secret of the fact that for some reason she had a mortal hatred for Ovid, and that she was apparently the driving force behind the Emperor's brutal decision.

Why?

Could it have been the revenge of a woman spurned, her impeccable reputation notwithstanding? Livia was fifteen years older than the poet, but such an age difference was of no greater consequence in Rome then than it would be now, especially if sex is an act of retaliation rather than affection. And could not Livia's hypothetical infidelity with the renowned poet have been just such an act of retaliation for her husband's dalliances with a variety of ladies of Rome, including perhaps the first wife of her lover?

But let us turn from speculation, and look at what the Questus manuscript can tell us about Ovid's destiny after his disappearance from Tomis. The attentive reader will have no problem concluding that Ovid left Tomis with the knowledge and permission of Poppaeus Sabinus, Tiberius's devoted and favored legate in Moesia and later in Macedonia.

The text contains several references to Proculeia's intercessions with Flaccus. This military man, later to become governor of Syria, was a personal friend of both Ovid (the poet addresses him in the *Black Sea Letters* Book 1.10) and the Emperor Tiberius. Flaccus and the latter shared a love of wine and questionable sexual indulgences. In fact, there are indications that his appointment to the Syrian governorship was less a compensation for his battlefield performance and more a favor to a friend who had spent long hours with the Emperor, partaking of alcohol and pederasty.

Further, Tiberius is commonly said to have so hated his own mother, Livia, that when the Senate suggested her posthumous deification and the construction of an arch in her memory, he quashed both proposals. After the demise of Augustus, who (apparently thanks to his wife) had remained unmoved with regard to Ovid, it would only make sense for Proculeia to ask them to intercede. Assuming, then, that Poppaeus acted with the tacit assent of Tiberius when he allowed Ovid to move to Vindobona, a place that had already grown from a military camp into a city with a thriving social life, and to a certain extent a center of culture as well, it seems evident that permission was granted on the condition that Ovid would "drown," and adopt a new name and biography. Hence his transformation from Ovid to Pomponius Pinnatus, and from the poet of *Metamorphoses* to the author of titillating comedy.

The fly in the poet's ointment, so to speak, was his old nemesis, Marcus Vesanius, who appeared unexpectedly in Vindobona (Scr. 4, Frg. 6) and attended a performance of Ovid's comedy (Scr. 4, Frg. 7). This was what drove the poet out of Vindobona.

Where did he find refuge?

The preserved fragments give only sketchy clues to his subsequent life. Governor Poppaeus—the man who established the official story of Ovid's death by drowning in Tomis—seems also to have helped him flee Vindobona in the company of Questus and Agricola. Two letters written by Poppaeus are mentioned in the text: one to Tiberius and the other to Cunobelinus.

The former probably would have contained Poppaeus's report to the Emperor that the troublesome poet had committed new and dangerous indiscretions in his refuge of Vindobona. After that, it was imperative that he be sent away from that city. The "drowning" and "resurrection" had apparently both been tacitly sanctioned by Tiberius (see Scr. 5, Frg. 1: "After all, Tiberius did agree").

But where to send him?

A clue is in the mention of the second letter,

to Cunobelinus. Cunobelinus (Shakespeare's *Cymbeline*) was a "king" of the Britons (*rex Britannorum*, as Suetonius described him) who was introducing Roman mores into pre-occupation England. For example, he minted coins with his own portrait; but more to the point, he cultivated the comforts of the court of Rome. This is understandable, for, according to Holinshed's sixteenth-century *Historie of England*, Cunobelinus (or, in Holinshed's spelling, Kymbeline) "was brought vp in Rome, and there made knight by Augustus Cesar, vnder whom he serued in the warres, and was in such fauour with him, that he was at libertie to pay his tribute or not." During his rule, there was vigorous trade with Roman garrisons in Germania and Gallia: in exchange for luxury items from Rome, Cunobelinus traded grain, hides, and iron, which the army needed above all, but also gold, silver, slaves, and hunting dogs.

In other words, life at Cunobelinus's court was a far cry from the primitive conditions in Tomis, and if Poppaeus chose Britain as the unfortunate poet's final destination it was a merciful, even generous, action: a British king with a Roman education would have known who Ovid was and in all probability had also read his works. Cunobelinus maintained contact with Roman culture and sent gifted youths to Rome for education and military training. Trade with his court was conducted by many larger and smaller Roman merchants; Questus mentions one (in Scr. 5, Frg. 1), who appears to have been the Charon who ferried Ovid to his ultimate home.

Still Ovid's friends did not give up.

Questus returned to Rome armed with the letter from Poppaeus, its contents still a mystery, since the seal had to remain unbroken, and he and Caecina once again approached the Emperor. There, of course, they "fared as badly as the legions at Teutoburg Forest" (Scr. 5, Frg. 2).

Certainly it would have been Livia's informer Marcus Vesanius who brought word of the poet's new comedy—perhaps even a copy of the script—to Rome. With this work, Ovid had almost certainly destroyed any chance he might have had of obtaining a pardon from Tiberius.

We don't know how long he lived in the court of King Cymbeline (if he ever did) or where and how he died. Nor do we know if he wrote any final work there, and if he did what form it took. It might have been a poem, or perhaps a tragedy like his *Medea*, which garnered great success in Rome but which also was not preserved.

✳ ✳ ✳

Now, let us focus on the second question raised by the Questus manuscript: How did Questus get to America?

He apparently sailed there on a ship known as a *moneris* (Scr. 7, Frg. 1), a single-banked galley also equipped in the Roman fashion with sails, but sails arranged in a system that enabled the ship to "maneuvre against the wind." No such system was known at the time, according to the sources, which leads to a conjecture that it might have been developed by Questus. Moreover, in Scr. 7, Frg. 2, we read that they "fully replenish[ed]" the ship's "stores of wood." Why would a ship with oars and sails need a supply of wood? For repairs? Questus makes no mention of any calamities occurring during the voyage that would have required extensive repairs. It appears, however, that the ship, well equipped with professional Greek oarsmen and a new system of sails, could be propelled even in a dead calm. We can deduce this from the scene described in the subsequent fragment (Scr. 7, Frg. 3): King Telalocus and his commanders and priests are gathered on the shore of the windless sea, observing "smoke rising straight up," and expecting "a volcano to rise from the sea." In the final fragment of the Questus manuscript, King Telalocus says, "But it is so far away. *Our* boats cannot get (there)" (the emphasis is mine).

The only logical conclusion is that Questus sailed to America on a ship powered by steam.

Granted, it does sound incredible: a steamship in the first century A.D.?

Some historians of technology speculate that, at the height of the Empire, Rome stood historically on the verge of discovering a power system to drive its military and other machines. Had it not been for the Empire's decline and fall, some Roman Wright brothers might have taken off in a flying machine by the end of the first millennium A.D. rather than a thousand years later. Of course, after Romulus

Augustulus, the last emperor, was deposed in A.D. 476, the situation in a Rome occupied by Germanic legions of its own once glorious army went from bad to worse. In the ensuing Christian centuries, only minuscule vestiges of the learning of classical civilization (and those mostly in the areas of the humanities) were preserved in monasteries. As for Roman technology, the only applications that survived were military ones like the onager.

Are there indications in Questus's text of how he could have arrived at the notion of something like the steam engine? There are. In Scr. 1, Frg. 11, in reply to the Emperor's question about what he planned to do with himself, the young Questus says, hesitantly, "I'd like to ... invent—for the army," but he is interrupted by his father's exclamation, "Toys! ... he thinks up toys!" The slave Sentris then brings in something that "stopped, when" something "slipped out." Regrettably, here again much of the manuscript is damaged to the point of complete illegibility, but whatever it was that Sentris brought, it apparently started moving, but then stopped— because something slipped out, *a part* of some sort.

Now let us look back to Scr. 1, Frg. 5, in which Proculeia's admirer Caecina brings little Questus a toy: three windmills made of tubes that "really spun (around)." In the history of technology, we find a record of something called Hero's aeolipile.

It is a toy, a closed metal vessel topped with two or four vertical tubes, bent at the ends. When the vessel is filled with water and hung over a fire, the water boils and the steam is forced out through the angled nozzles, making the vessel rotate. In short, an early precursor to the steam engine, or more precisely, the steam turbine. No one took it very seriously—a mere toy, as the father Gaius correctly referred to it.

Sources attribute the invention of this device to Hero of Alexandria, whose fame culminated around A.D. 65, and who developed other such mechanisms. Assuming the genuineness of the Questus manuscript, and it has been confirmed by experts, the toy was clearly known as far back as the end of the first century B.C., but neither at that time nor three-quarters of a century later in Hero's time did anyone think of applying it to anything but the entertainment of children.

But what was the part that "slipped out" and caused the thing to stop?

In order for the power of an aeolipile to drive some sort of vehicle—and that appears to be what Questus was demonstrating for the Emperor—it had to have some sort of mechanical transmission component to turn the wheels.

Aside from his other notable qualities (e.g., a talent for writing well in the Latin of the time of Augustus), Questus was perceptive. One thing we know he noticed was an unconscious mannerism that afflicted Caecina: whenever that diffident suitor of Proculeia was embarrassed or ill at ease, "he would rock his interlaced fingers up and down, repeatedly" with "fingers intertwined," and Questus remarks, "Later I often (recalled) that image" (Scr. 1, Frg. 9).

Questus obviously had an excellent technical imagination, and the movement of Caecina's inter- twined fingers may have suggested to him the work- ings of a device involving meshed gears, of the sort we know from the early fourth century A.D., used in mills to transform water power into the rotary movement of the grinding mechanism.

In the toy, such a device might have been capable of driving the miniature wheels of some diminutive vehicle. Still, no matter how much improved, one wonders how it would have sufficed to propel a steam-powered ship. Questus, however, was an amaz- ingly creative young man. We need only look back to Scr. 2, Frg. 1 (and also to Scr. 3, Frg. 12), for the description of the battle with the army of Dalmatian commander Bato. Questus writes: "Impressed, I observed how the skirmishers streamed back between the maniples of the first, second, and third lines, moving through the gaps like water flowing through some multi-channel aqueduct." Watching the move- ments of the legions, Questus has "a strong sense of some significance in what I was seeing, a signifi- cance specific to me. I shivered," he continues, "not with fear, but with some sort of elation," and, "instead of the battle," he saw "the solution that would enable the transfer of the rotational force to"—and while here the manuscript is once again illegible, the fragment concludes with "all the components of the legion worked like—and once again, I thought of that word," but the word that follows is also illegible. However, it can be extrapolated from the context: the word is "machine," the Roman military machine by means of which Rome often defeated armies that were numerically superior but fought in a "barbarian"—i.e., disorderly and uncoordinated—manner. When we read Questus commenting on the operation of this "machine" in Scr. 2, Frg. 1, we can see clearly how the regular backward and forward flow of soldiers through the precisely ordered gaps between the maniples could lead his fertile young imagination to an idea that would occur seventeen centuries later to James Watt.

Fantastic? Perhaps. But every inventor needs to fantasize. Other fragments of the manuscript certainly confirm that Questus had the requisite creative spark. In Scr. 3, Frg. 1, for example, Agricola, himself an accomplished smith, says, "I don't entirely understand … functions," said Agricola, "but Questus is brilliant...." A bit further on, Scr. 3, Frg. 12, contains a concept that much later would be crucial to Watts's invention: "and an opening here. The trick is that when the valve slides under it, it draws...." Once again, we run into critical gaps in the text; however, the word "valve" reappears a few lines later, when the smith Agricola remarks appreciatively, "it's a brilliant idea, Questus. But the valve will have to be forged like a sword, tempered...."

Thinking imaginatively, as Questus would have, let us accept the hypothesis that a young Roman could have come up with a steam engine. Might he, then, have used it to drive his ship, on a windless sea, all the way to American shores? We know from his own words that, long before Columbus but in accord with the teaching of the most learned Greek philosophers, Questus believed that the world is round. Consider, for example, his exchange with Cornelius Fidus in Scr. 6, Frg. 2, and the astonishment of King Telalocus looking at the full moon (Scr. 7, Frg. 5) and saying, "You say that is what the earth is like?"

It is a historical fact that the first recorded steamboats were paddle-wheelers. Would Questus's vessel have been equipped with a paddle wheel? There is no description of the ship in the text, but it is my considered opinion that it would not. Such a propulsion device would have had to be mounted in the stern, as they were on the steamboats on the Mississippi, to be out of the way of the oarsmen. It is not impossible, but in my opinion, Questus's ship did not utilize a paddle wheel. My evidence for this conclusion may seem slight, but I believe it is sufficient. It is contained in the youthful Questus's observations of another toy, also a gift from the enamoured Caecina.

The brief, fragmentary description (Scr. 1, Frg. 2) refers to it as the "(wings) of Icarus," which "did not resemble wings at all but did in fact fly. It was a round stick topped perpendicularly with two thin flat pieces of ... When twirled between one's (palms) ..." This is all we learn about the "wings of Icarus," but even today there is a similar child's flying toy, equipped with horizontal blades. It flies on the basis of the fact that air is matter, and its rotating blades, in fact a propeller, screw themselves into the air. To my knowledge, there is no reference to the original toy anywhere in historical literature, but once again, I rest my conclusions on the veracity of the Questus manuscript.

Questus's steamship was driven by a propeller.

This concludes my commentary. The remainder of the text is sufficiently clear, or is clarified in the notes.

LETTER FROM
MR. ANDRÉ FOUILLET

*When the first edition of this book was published by
Nary & Trace Publishers in New York, the editor-in-chief received a letter from Monsieur André Fouillet,
which we append in recognition of its relevance to this
second edition. My commentary follows.*

Dear Editor,
It was with interest that I read the book *The Narrative
of Questus Firmus Siculus*, published by your firm in
the translation of the eminent Professor Howard
Phillips Langhorn and with commentary from the pen
of Mr. Patrick Oliver Enfield, famous author of, for
the most part, detective mysteries and horror stories.

The archaic character of the writing and of the
material on which Questus Firmus Siculus wrote has
been studied by a number of distinguished scholarly
commissions, all of which concurred, positively
dating the manuscript to the mid–first century A.D.
and unanimously confirming its authenticity. In his
fascinating commentary, Mr. P. O. Enfield hypothe-
sizes convincingly that a Latin manuscript from the
time of the first two Caesars could, if a certain
sequence of events had taken place, have found its
way to a complex of Mayan structures in Copán,

which structures demonstrably could only have come into being after the year A.D. 400.

Mr. Enfield, then, has given us a satisfactory answer to the question of how the manuscript arrived at the site where it was uncovered by Miskatonic University students of Mayan architecture, under the guidance of Professor Langhorn. While I myself am not a scholar—I am in fact an accountant by profession—I have since my early youth had an avocation: not a single week of my life has passed without a visit to the theater. I am particularly fond of comedies and farces by French authors of the nineteenth century. One might describe me as an *amateur*, in the sense of a lover, of such theater.

Perhaps because I *am* such a lover, I noticed an enigma in the Questus narrative, unexplained and apparently overlooked by both Mr. Enfield and Professor H. P. Langhorn. I refer to the brief, perplexing fragment of a comedy, ostensibly (according to Questus Firmus Siculus) written by Publius Ovidius Naso. It so happens that the writings of this poet are my other passion.

To Questus it seems that Ovid's *trabeata* casts light on Caesar Augustus's reason for sentencing the poet to lifelong exile in Tomis on the Black Sea. It is a fact that no scholar or author has been able to determine the actual ground of this banishment, neither Dio Cassius (born A.D. 155) nor contemporary academicians like Hermann Fränkel or L. P. Wilkinson, or any others in the time between these two. Some, for example A. D. Fitton Brown (as cited by Mr. Enfield), even disallow Ovid's sojourn in Tomis altogether. Because only a tiny scrap of the comedy has survived the ages, certainly not enough for us to deduce the Caesar's motivation, the matter of Ovid's *relegatio* remains, regrettably, unclarified.

However, the fragment amazed me. It enfolds yet another mystery. Compare, if you will, the following two texts. One is from Act I of a farce entitled *La Puce à l'oreille* (*A Flea in Her Ear*), a work of Georges Feydeau, French playwright of the turn of the nineteenth and twentieth centuries. The Ovid text is from Fragment 3 in Scroll 5 of the *Narrative*. Under each rejoinder from Ovid's play, the corresponding rejoinder in Feydeau is in italics. I have parenthesized those sections in the Feydeau that are not found in the text allegedly by Ovid.

> Such stamina? Really? Such a constitution!
> FINACHE: (*Insurance companies are ridiculously inquisitive. But I must congratulate you. What a husband you have, madame!*) *What a constitution! What stamina!*

FURNILLA: Indeed!
> LUCIENNE: *Don't I know it!*

CAPITO: You are to be congratulated.
> FINACHE: *It's very flattering.*

FURNILLA: But do you know how tiring it is?
> LUCIENNE: *But exhausting!*

CAPITO: Well, you can't have everything.
  FINACHE: *You get nothing without working for it in this world.*

PLAUTUS: It is what Lentilla dreams of.
  ETIENNE: *It's what Madame Plucheux dreams about.*

FURNILLA: Who is that?
  LUCIENNE: *Who on earth's that?*

PLAUTUS: My concubine. I'm not enough for her. What she needs is a man like Gaius Invalidus Sicanus.
  ETIENNE: *My wife. Too much for me. I can tell you, she needs a man like madame's husband.*

CAPITO: Well then, with your permission, Furnilla, and of course, if Gaius is willing.
  FINACHE: *Then with madame's permission and the Spanish gentleman's consent (—the thing might be arranged!)*

You will surely grant, sir, that the differences between the two texts are to all intents and purposes negligible, and mostly—if we can trust the fidelity of the English translators—of a purely linguistic nature, the language of Feydeau being more literary, that of Ovid more conversational. However, both passages speak with great frankness, under the lightest of veils, about sex.

In Ovid's piece, Plautus is apparently a slave, whose name the author borrowed from the great

Roman dramatist who lived at the turn of the third and second centuries B.C., and whose comedies usually contain the character of a wily slave. Etienne in Feydeau's farce is a remote cousin to that stock character in the plays of Plautus, whom the Roman had himself borrowed from the comedies of his Greek precursors. According to Mr. Enfield's commentaries, Capito is Ovid himself. Furnilla, whose husband's name is Gaius Invalidus Sicanus, could be Livia, wife to Caesar Augustus (as Mr. Enfield presumes in his note). Augustus suffered poor health most of his life and twice fell so ill that his survival was in doubt. Hence perhaps the *nomen* (one that I cannot find listed in the literature as one in common use) Invalidus.

But how can the play be made to explain Ovid's banishment from Rome? Feydeau's farce, typically for this author, is a tangled tale revolving around a more or less virtuous wife who suspects her more or less virtuous husband of infidelity. Caesar Augustus was indeed said to be a womanizer, and the title *The Faithful Husband* could be meant sarcastically, if of course Invalidus was intended to represent Augustus. The Empress Livia, on the other hand—and this in my opinion makes Mr. Enfield's hypothesis about her relationship with Ovid untenable—is known to have been faithful beyond reproach and supremely virtuous, setting aside the murders she almost certainly committed to obtain for Tiberius, her son by her first marriage, the right of succession to the throne.

As I indicated at the beginning of this letter, I am no scholar, merely a student and lover of French comedy and Ovid's erotic poetry. Perhaps those more erudite than I will come up with some plausible explanation for this conundrum. I admit that I am at a loss to explain it.

Are you absolutely certain that the entire thing is not a hoax?

Respectfully yours,

André Fouillet

P. O. ENFIELD'S COMMENTS

T he similarities between the two scenes are indisputable. How can this be? The only possible explanation is the unsatisfactory one of coincidence. Feydeau could not have had access to the Questus scrolls. I admit it is rather like claiming that two men, having tossed words cut out of a newspaper into a hat, then reached in and drew out identical words in the identical order, and thus assembled identical texts by coincidence. But how else am I to explain it, accepting as I do the conclusive and irrefutable authenticity of the Questus script?

M. Fouillet is correct in his statement that Ovid's scene is as open about sex as his *Amores* and his *Art of Love*, and that the name of the husband whose wife complains of his formidable potency can be interpreted as a reference to Augustus's perpetual infirmities. Similarly, we can equate the name Capito with Ovid's *cognomen*, Naso, since they both refer to body parts, and both above the shoulders at that. If we take what is preserved of the scene as a more or less realistic depiction of the relationship between the Empress, the poet, and the infirm but superpotent Emperor, we can surely presume that it attributes Ovid's *relegatio* to matters sexual.

Absurd as it may seem, I am tempted to look to Feydeau's farce for an answer to the enigma of Ovid's life. The classic French play is about a bunch of bourgeois Parisians setting out to commit adultery, not one of whom, over the entire course of the play, is successful; the dominant motif of the farce is "a string of errors." In Ovid's poems from exile he himself refers cryptically to the reason for his banishment as "*carmen et error*," i.e., "poem and error," as it is generally translated. Scholars have concluded that the error committed by the poet was probably that of not reporting improprieties that he had witnessed. Still, let us not forget—if I remember my Lyceum Latin correctly—the Latin *error* can also be translated as "misunderstanding," or "blunder."

But this is all sheer fantasy. The apparent bit of Feydeau in Ovid's text is as mysterious as the dark motive that led the Emperor to cunningly condemn Ovid to death by grief.

A LETTER FROM
HERR RUDOLF CEEH

The first editions of this book were quite successful, and as a result it was translated into a number of languages. After the publication of the German edition, I received this letter. Realizing at once the interest it would hold for readers of Questus's Narrative, *I had it translated into English for this third edition.*

Dear Mr. Enfield,

After reading the *Narrative of Questus*, and above all your commentary on this amazing, improbable manuscript, whose authenticity has nonetheless been confirmed by experts, I have decided to send you the enclosed German translation of a certain Latin manuscript, also from the early Roman Empire, and to tell you how it came into my possession. Unlike the Questus manuscript, it has never been submitted to experts for confirmation of its authenticity. Should you, however, find it worthy of expert scrutiny, I can arrange for you to examine the original.

I purchased it in 1987, in the antique shop of Herr Otto Reimann, on Himmelsbütteler Weg, which at that time was in the western sector of the divided city of Berlin. It was later translated from Latin into German by Eva Althammer, Ph.D., Professor of Classical Languages at the State Lyceum in Düsseldorf, where I was her pupil before being conscripted into the army during the war. The enclosed is the translated text as she dictated it to me.

I am no authority on the Latin language—my knowledge is limited to the vestiges of my schoolboy mastery of that beautiful tongue. Nor am I an authority on antiques, with the exception of the very narrow field of old (and some more modern) tin soldiers. Until my retirement in 1985, I was director of operations of Michaela Swinkels & Co., becoming also, in 1983, part owner. The firm, a toy factory situated in West Berlin, always did very well, and continues to do so, and thus I find myself very well provided for in my old age. My wife passed on back in 1970, and as our marriage was childless I am now at liberty to devote myself almost entirely to my hobby, collecting the aforementioned tin soldiers. I have quite a respectable collection of almost ten thousand of these figures, from Frederick the Great's "tall fellows" to a little-known complete set depicting Adolf Hitler reviewing his personal bodyguard unit, the *Adolf Hitler Leibstandarte*. The peculiarity of this set is that the Führer's arm is hinged at the shoulder to enable it to be raised in the Aryan salute.

When I discovered Herr Reimann's store in 1987, it was an antique shop in name only. At the time, the proprietor was eighty-nine years old (he died shortly thereafter) and his store resembled nothing so much as what in America they call a junk shop: a jumble of old, broken, and apparently worthless furniture, dented brass instruments and stringless violins, dusty tuxedos and other musty refuse. And yet among all this scrap I made an astonishing find: an almost complete and extremely rare mid-eighteenth-century set of figures of the Roman legionaries defeated in the Teutoburg Forest by the German Cheruscans under Prince Arminius. Naturally, this discovery inspired me to spend almost an entire day searching Herr Reimann's establishment for other such treasures. Just when I had finally decided to give it up, something caught my eye. The shop walls were covered with faded prints and mangy, antlered trophies accumulated by generations of deer hunters, but for some reason, my attention was caught by something in a black frame, a picture or perhaps a diploma—it was hard to tell through the layers of dirt and dust. I stepped closer to whatever it was and rubbed the glass with my handkerchief until I could discern what was behind it. No diploma, but no picture either; rather, an old, handwritten text, not in German *Schwabacher* script. I still retain enough of the classics I read during my school days to be able to recognize the Latin language, but unfortunately, my efforts with the handkerchief sufficed only to uncover here and there a word or phrase.

I asked the venerable proprietor where he had acquired the document, which might well be of interest. He approached the frame and peered at it through his thick glasses. Then he said, "Some fellow sold it to me, but I can't recollect his name. It was a lot of years ago. Before the Wall. He had whiskers all around his face." Herr Reimann indicated with his index finger the location and appearance of the man's beard. "I have another one in the back. There were three of them, but the glass got broken on the one and when I was removing the shards the telephone rang, so I rested my cigar on the frame—I was still smoking cigars then—and went out into the shop where the telephone was. By the time I got back, the cigar had rolled off the frame and the paper was burning. Well, I put out the fire with water from the tea kettle but all that was left were scorched shreds. I tossed them out."

At the time, I had no idea how great a loss his carelessness had caused, but a loss it undoubtedly was. I asked him, "Have you read what was written on it?"

"No, sir. It's in Latin. I used to have a passable knowledge of Latin, but ever since my stroke, it seems to have faded from my memory. They tell me that's common. It certainly happened to me."

When I asked him if I could take a look at the other framed text, he disappeared into the back room; after a time he shuffled back with it in his arms. It was in even worse condition than the one on the wall. The glass was covered with an accumulation of dust and flyspecks, with some sticky, oily stuff spilled on it, maybe axle grease. I wiped away what I could and a word became visible, clearly in Latin—*castra*.

"How much?" I asked.

He had asked a mere hundred marks for the set of massacred legionaries. He had obviously lost any sense of pricing he might once have had. He thought for a while, and then said, "Twenty marks. For the two of them."

I paid him, and with the Roman soldiers in my satchel and the two framed documents under my arm, I flagged a taxi and went home.

Later, as I was preparing to remove the documents from their frames to get a closer look at them, I was pleasantly surprised. Printed in pencil, on the back of both documents, were the words:

PROPERTY OF HELMUT SCHELLENDORF
SCHLUMPENGASSE

Herr Schellendorf had not troubled to put his house number, and I had no idea where Schlumpengasse might be. But I was elated by the good fortune of having found my miniature Roman paladins, and I did not doubt for a moment that if this Helmut Schellendorf was still alive, I would find him. Once I had extracted the documents from the frame I tried to read the text. All I succeeded in doing, however, was to reconfirm for myself the fact that, although I had not yet suffered a stroke, my Latin was also extremely rusty. And to think that I had once been Dr. Althammer's star pupil!

The few phrases I could decipher suggested that it was the record of some military encounter, and the number at the end of the manuscript apparently dated the document: CCCMLXXXIV, that is, the year 784. Startled, I realized for the first time that the document was over a thousand years old. Looking closer, I made out, with difficulty, the letters A-U-C. After a moment, from somewhere in the depths of my memory of the charming professor's Latin classes, the words AB URBE CONDITA floated up and arranged themselves in front of my mind's eye. From the founding of the city.

Not A.D. 784. This text was dated according to the Roman calendar numbering the years since the founding of Rome in 753 B.C. The manuscript, if it was authentic, was written in the year A.D. 31. It was almost *two* thousand years old!

A quiver of excitement went up my spine. I remembered hearing that some of the inks used in ancient Rome had survived the ages if they had been applied to high-quality papyrus scrolls. My excitement gradually gave way to triumph as I came to suspect that for a trifling twenty marks, I might have purchased a priceless treasure. And only then did I reflect on how great a loss doddering old Herr Reimann had carelessly caused by burning the third document.

Carefully, I replaced the scrolls inside the glass frames that had protected them for the last hundred years or so, wrapped them securely in heavy brown paper and put them in my suitcase. Then I drove to Düsseldorf to see Professor Eva Althammer, Ph.D.

She lived in an outlying area of the city, in a charming cottage built many years ago by her late husband, the school trustee Alfred Althammer. Inside the cottage, which had survived the war, everything was as pleasant as I remembered, from the days when I used to visit my professor there on the pretext of seeking guidance in a translation of the six elegies of Lygdamus, from the third book of Albius Tibullus.

My revered professor passionately believed that the poems had in fact come from the pen of Tibullus himself. I was translating them as an extracurricular labour of love, not so much for the poet as for his devotee. Sadly, I was called up before I finished and never returned to the Lygdamus elegies, forgetting, even without the benefit of a stroke, almost all of that splendid dead language. But I had not forgotten my professor's mellow voice, which had read aloud to a rapt audience of seventeen-year-olds the (somewhat expurgated) poems of Ovid, describing an activity that no one before him had perceived as art.

Of course, while I had forgotten an appalling amount of that wonderful extinct tongue, the professor had not.

She welcomed me in the doorway of her little, ivy-covered house, slender and with hardly a trace of a stoop, amazingly energetic and alert for her ninety-two years. I had last visited her when she turned ninety, and she had not changed a bit. Not that I was surprised. I have always believed that people who live to such an advanced age are blessed by God with an indestructible constitution, so that death must sneak up on them: they die in an auto accident or from a spoiled oyster.

"Ah, Rudy! Welcome, my boy! Good heavens, can this mean you've kept your promise?" At her ninetieth-birthday gathering, with all her surviving pupils in attendance—unfortunately only a very few, if you don't count the girls—she had recalled my attempt at translating Lygdamus. Rashly, I promised to finish the job. And I did give it a try, but since I couldn't find a translation in the library, and had long lost my crib sheet on Lygdamus, I made no headway.

"I'm sorry, Professor, that isn't it. What I mean is, I had the best of intentions, but by sheer coincidence I have happened upon something even more fascinating—if you'll forgive me—than Lygdamus."

She nodded, a little reproachfully, and invited me in. Seating herself on the beautifully preserved old Biedermeier settee, she gestured to me to resume my old place, on a loveseat dating back to some Louis or other.

Apologetically, I continued, "I understand that you may see this as a betrayal of our erstwhile project. But you must appreciate that what I found in a Berlin antique shop is either an extremely well-crafted and impressive fraud, or a unique find: a Latin manuscript from the first century AD."

"It is far more likely to be the former. After all, how could such a treasure have survived in one of Berlin's well-scoured antique shops? What is the subject of the manuscript?"

Sheepishly, I told her that I had not properly perused the text, in part because I had not been able to decipher the ancient script, and that this was the reason for my visit.

"Hmm," she said. "Let me see it."

I took the package from my suitcase and removed the two scrolls from their glass enclosure. The professor took them, and without putting on a pair of spectacles—of course, she didn't need them—she placed the scrolls on the coffee table, and immediately started reading. After a while, she looked up and declared indignantly, "There was no island called Tesalus in the Roman Empire. It is a hoax."

"Could you translate a bit of it for me, Professor?" I asked, shamefaced.

She gave me a another sharp look. "Do you mean to say that even something this simple is too much for you now?"

Shaking her head, she turned back to the text and began translating, smoothly and skilfully, in the same mellow voice I remembered. But this was no poetry. As she continued, effortlessly translating at sight, her old housekeeper entered the room, bringing us a tray of coffee and cakes. I took the opportunity to take out the writing paper and pen I had brought with me, and asked the professor to dictate the text to me.

In an hour, we were finished. I didn't know what to think.

"Well," she asked in a significant tone, "What do you say *now*?"

I wasn't sure what she was implying. After a moment, I hazarded, "It's certainly interesting. It's very unfortunate, of course, that the middle section is missing, but as I told you, Herr Reimann accidentally destroyed it—"

With something like sad derision in her blue eyes, she said, "You are not particularly well versed in literature, are you?"

I admitted to having forgotten a lot. "But I remember a lot too. Lucretius: *De rerum natura, Aeneis, Ars*—"

She interrupted, "I am not speaking of Latin literature." Again she paused, then delivered her verdict: "A clear hoax. Written in excellent Latin, but a hoax nonetheless."

I was crushed. I had no doubt she was right. Still, I couldn't get it out of my head, and as I drove home, I went over and over the long list of unanswered questions.

Who was Helmut Schellendorf? How had he come by this fraudulent manuscript and why had he sold it to Herr Reimann? Could he be some old Latin scholar, living on a measly pittance of a pension and improving his lot by selling off worthless belongings? Or had he, with his profound knowledge of Latin, manufactured this text as some sort of practical joke? A joke on whom? Or perhaps to sell it as an oddity? Or an actual swindle? If so, it had not been a success; Herr Reimann could not have paid much for it, even if, as he said, he had bought it a long time ago and had no clear recollection of the seller.

I searched the map of Berlin for Schlumpengasse, but was unsuccessful. Then I recalled that Herr Reimann said he had bought it "before the Wall." In those days, although the East was communist and part of another country, crossing the city from east to west had been as simple as getting on the underground on one side and getting off on the other. (As it is again, thank God, now that the Wall is gone.)

Things began to make sense. Could Herr Schellendorf have been an East Berlin pensioner, selling his possessions in West Berlin for hard

currency? Such currency went much further than
East German marks toward maintaining a household.
My city map was from 1977, and showed no
Schlumpengasse. Then it occurred to me. Of course!
The administration of East Berlin had constantly
rewarded its many "heroes of labour" with the osten-
sible immortality of having streets renamed after them.

On a 1932 map from the library, I found
Schlumpengasse. This was not very helpful, but it
did show it to be an avenue in Berlin-Pankow, and by
comparing the old map with my newer one I determined that the street in question had in fact been
renamed Heinrich Poltergeiststrasse. Trying to find a
Helmut Schellendorf, who did not list a house
number, on that long Pankow thoroughfare in hostile,
foreign territory (I remind you, Herr Enfield, that
this was in 1987) promised to be an unpleasant if
not downright risky operation. A fellow going house
to house asking after a citizen of East Germany would
be unlikely to escape the attention of the various
"voluntary" collaborators with the Stasi secret police,
and that less than God-fearing organization would
surely give him a serious going over.

I had almost decided to simply forget about the
unknown Latin scholar and his practical joke, but my
eyes were still on the map, and I noticed a side street
that intersected Comrade Poltergeist's avenue diago-
nally: Kastanienallee, Chestnut Lane. It recalled to
my mind a factory on that street with which the firm
of Michaela Swinkels had done business for years.
They had supplied us with cheap lathes and milling

machines, not by any stretch of the imagination up to West German standards, but certainly good enough for our manufacture of children's metal building sets and toy steam locomotives. And the price had been right. It was one of those East German anomalies, a small private enterprise that continued to operate well into the 1950s. We later found an even less expensive supplier in South Africa, though, and the arrangement ended. I had not thought of the factory since then, and had no idea what became of it.

Its name had been Metallbauwerke Zimmermann & Schilling, and when I turned to the East German Commerce Bureau for information, they told me that it was now called the Ernst Erdpflügerwerke, apparently a nationalized business, because when I asked—naively—who Ernst Erdpflüger was, I was told that he was a long-dead hero of the workers who had been an active figure in the Cooperative Movement. I explained to the bureaucrat that my company had once done business with Herr Zimmermann—they knew all about that, of course—and that the daughter of its late proprietor, Frau Michaela Swinkels-Kristenson, would like to re-establish commercial relations. So she would be happy if they could grant me a visa, because, although I was already retired, I had been the one responsible for our earlier commercial relationship with the firm. It was a week before they complied, but eventually my visa was issued.

In the Eastern Zone, I encountered another surprise.

I was received at the Erdpflügerwerke by its executive director, whose name—Horst Sepp Klinkenglocker (his parents must have admired the *Horst Wessel Lied* and the well-known SS commander Sepp Dietrich)—bespoke a non-Communist past. His present position, however, had clearly necessitated a radical shift to "comrade." His vocabulary too was in keeping with that position. It was certainly not the language of Goethe. I briefly considered asking after Helmut Schellendorf, but I decided that the executive director was not the right man to ask, and that showing too great an interest in pre-war employees might jeopardize my peaceful old age. A very few words with Herr Klinkenglocker, in fact, proved him to be the model of an expert socialist factory manager: he was totally ignorant about the manufacture of lathes and milling machines, and even less informed on international commercial dealings. So I had no difficulty convincing him that my visit was a preliminary one, merely to determine whether the Erdpflügerwerke enterprise might be interested in rekindling commercial relations. I would be returning shortly with concrete proposals. That said, I asked the director if he would kindly show me around the factory, so that I might refresh old memories.

I still had no idea how to ask after Helmut Schellendorf.

The factory had not changed at all since I had last visited it some thirty years earlier, when it had already been operating with antiquated, pre-war equipment. As we moved through the spacious old turning shop (of course, Herr Klinkenglocker informed me, officiously, that this was the turning shop), I spied a man I recognized from the old days of Zimmermann & Schilling. Back then he had been a young foreman; now, still sitting in his old spot in the foreman's cubicle, he was a familiar figure despite the thirty extra years, the grey hair, and the beer belly.

"Herr Gleichschalter!" I exclaimed, sounding pleasantly surprised, which in fact I was. "Is it really you?" Turning to Klinkenglocker, whose ears were twitching, I remarked, "I remember Herr Gleichschalter from the old days when he was in charge of our orders," and, to the old foreman, "I'm pleased to see you alive and well."

"I am that, thank God, Herr Ceeh."

Klinkenglocker interrupted, clumsily attempting to show off how well he knew his operation, saying, "Comrade Gleichschalter has been with us for all of fifteen years!"

Mildly, Gleichschalter corrected him: "Thirty-five years, Comrade Director."

He and I chatted for a while, with Klinkenglocker breaking in with occasional blundering interjections, which Gleichschalter would laconically set right. After a while I asked, as if by the by, "Is Herr Schellendorf still working here?"

The foreman frowned as he searched his memory.

"He was...." I began, then stopped short as I realized I had no idea what Schellendorf looked like. I changed my tack. "He was a lathe operator, if memory serves. It's been a long time...."

It was, admittedly, a shot in the dark, and Gleichschalter was shaking his head when Herr Klinkenglocker broke in, pleased to display some information that the foreman could not contradict. "Schellendorf, you say? I think he wrote us recently with some request or other."

We went into his office, where his secretary looked in a card file and confirmed that Herr Schellendorf had paid them a visit. "He was asking us for a letter of confirmation that he used to work here, in support of his application for a place in a pensioners' home." She glanced again at the card. "He used to work in the pressing shop."

"Of course! The pressing shop!" I exclaimed joyfully. "I would so like to see my old friend! Do you have his address?"

I felt safe in assuming that an old codger applying for placement in a retirement home would not be of any interest to the Stasi. Of course, I was thinking like a citizen of the West.

The secretary had come up with an address. "Number 9 Heinrich Poltergeiststrasse," she read out to me, and I wrote it down.

Luckily, the bombs had spared the house at 9 Heinrich Poltergeiststrasse, and no repairs had been done on it since the end of the war. It was a shabby two-storey building with a shop on the ground floor, its display window no cleaner than the glass that had obscured the text by the alleged Questus Firmus Siculus. The sun-faded sign above the window read SHOE REPAIRS, and whoever had hung it hadn't bothered to remove the old, taller sign, so the top half of the name of the former proprietor was still visible. I guessed it to be ERICH MITTENBERG, SHOEMAKER.

I walked into the shop and found, sitting on a stool at a cobbler's bench mending an old brogue, a person who was apparently the selfsame Erich Mittenberg. I estimated his age to be about that of the antique dealer—around eighty. I addressed him, "I'm looking for Herr Helmut Schellendorf."

"You'll have to go across the hall," said the shoemaker. "I'd call him over, but poor Helmut doesn't get around any more. He applied for a wheelchair way back, five years ago, but never got it. So now he's applying for a nursing home."

I watched the old tradesman, still hammering away at shoes in the dingy shop that once had been his own. I asked, "If he had a wheelchair, would he be able to stay at home?"

"Of course he would. Then he could get to the grocery store on his own, and not have to rely on old Frau Treppenhäuser to bring him something. Come on, I'll take you to him."

He got down and hobbled over to a door in the side wall of his tiny workshop. I recognized the hobble. He belonged to the large German contingent of war veterans walking on prostheses.

We crossed the narrow corridor, and Mittenberg banged on a door opposite, calling, "Helmut! You have a visitor."

"Well, what do you know," came a cheery voice from behind the door. "Dietrich?"

Mittenberg opened the door. "No. It's some gentleman." His eyes assessed my suit. "From the West, correct?" He turned to leave.

A round-faced man was resting on a decrepit sofa, his rosy cheeks framed by the short beard of a sailor. In the corner of the room was a bed, its rarely washed sheets in disarray. On the wall beside the couch a picture clipped from a magazine had been tacked to the wall. It depicted a submarine with its crew standing at attention on the deck; the flag on the commander's turret in the photograph had been blacked out.

"Have a seat, sir," the sailor urged me amiably. "Here, take the footstool, it's the only seat in the house."

I sat down to a war story that was simply amazing. And God knows I've heard a lot of them.

Herr Schellendorf had served in Hitler's navy during the war. To be precise, he was a mechanic on the submarine UB 1809-49. The war's end found him in the South Atlantic, where his U-boat was more likely hiding than on the lookout for Allied ships. In mid-June of 1945, the submarine's captain and his officers decided to surrender the vessel to the brand new "Allied" (though until that spring they had been officially neutral) government of General Perón. Helmut Schellendorf disagreed—he would by far have preferred to sail back to Hamburg and trust to the gentlemanliness of the Brits, who were administering the occupied port there—but obedience was bred in his bones, and so he obeyed. Before the war he had apprenticed as a machinist with the

Metallbauwerke Zimmermann & Schilling in Berlin-
Pankow, where he lived with his elderly mother. Then
he married, and his young wife died giving birth to
their first child, which lived only a few hours.
Schellendorf, devastated, enlisted in the newly established German navy with the vague intention of
seeking restful death in some distant sea. That was
in 1935, and his background led them to assign him
to submarines. He was always interested in things
mechanical, so he did not object, and he was happy
there, at least until the war.

Helmut Schellendorf was no Nazi. He liked beer,
kids, dogs, cats, and his trade, and remained immune
to the temptations of the various political movements
of the times that were buttering up the working
classes. But because obedience was in his bones,
Schellendorf just clicked his heels when Captain
Hans von Kressinger (who, unlike his mechanic, was
a Nazi) decided that the submarine would surrender
in Buenos Aires. Instead of interning the crew in
camps, the friendly government offered them work
according to their rank and experience. Schellendorf
was employed in a locksmith's shop on Avenida Jesú,
and spent his spare time down at the docks, going
from ship to ship, trying to find one that would take
him back to Germany.

He finally found one in the spring of 1946, and
that May he landed in Hamburg. By good luck he
was able to get past all the checkpoints in the port
and board a train for Berlin, where he hoped to find
his mother still alive. He found the house, untouched

by the bombs, but his mother was with the angels.
He had no difficulty, though, getting re-employed at
his old plant, the Metallbauwerke Zimmermann &
Schilling, which had also escaped damage and was
just resuming production. He was working in the same
shop when Zimmermann & Schilling became the Ernst
Erdpflügerwerke, and he remained there until 1956,
when severe rheumatism forced him to retire prematurely on an invalid's pension. When I met him, he had
given up hope of ever being allotted a wheelchair, and
had instead filed for a spot in an old people's home,
in hopes of being accepted there within the decade.

Surprisingly, the troubles, tragedies, thrills, and
political turnabouts of his life hadn't made a pessimist
of him; on the contrary, he had become a jocular old
man. His defense against misfortune was gallows
humor, and his life as he described it had been an
endless farce on the sea, under the sea, under Perón
and his beautiful wife, and then under the workers'
state, to which he ultimately became useless when
rheumatism confined him to this settee. Like most
Germans who had lived through the war and the
various trappings of Hitler's state (which were by
then starting to fade into improbability) only to find
themselves under the rule of Communists, he was
resigned to hardships reminiscent more of the tales of
the brothers Grimm than of real life. So far nothing
out of the ordinary.

I asked Schellendorf how the Latin manuscript
that he had sold to Herr Reimann had come into his
possession.

"I'll tell you about that too," he said, "but you don't have a little tobacco on you, do you?" He held out a charred pipe, desperately empty.

I didn't, but I had noticed a smoke shop on the corner. I returned with a plentiful supply, enough to last him a month or more. I used to be a pipe smoker, and I was dubious about the quality: when Schellendorf exhaled his first puff of smoke, it didn't smell of violets. He seemed happy with it, though, and I urged him to proceed with the history of that hoax.

He began the tale. "I brought it home in the same bottle I found it in. I showed it to Dietrich Kunstmann. He and I went to grade school together, except he went on to the lyceum, and he told me it was Latin. He couldn't tell me what it said, because he was expelled for moral delinquency when he was fourteen, but he told me it was probably valuable, so I had it framed to keep it from getting damaged and hung it on my wall. That was when I still lived in the one-bedroom flat upstairs, where I had plenty of wall space."

"What did you do with the bottle?"

"I threw it out. It wouldn't open, it was sealed tight with something that no corkscrew could penetrate, so I broke it off at the neck to see what was inside. I didn't do that till I got home, though. I thought there might be a model ship inside it, the kind they sell in harbours. Old sailors make them, glue them together out of boredom. They do it through the neck of the bottle, something incredible."

"Couldn't you see inside?"

"No, the glass was dark, green or black, you couldn't tell anything through it."

"But instead of a model ship you found a manuscript."

"Yes." Schellendorf nodded. "And when I couldn't make ends meet on my invalid pension, I sold it to Herr Reimann. For thirty marks."

So old Reimann had only lost ten marks on the deal.

For a while, we were silent. Herr Schellendorf relit his pipe. Then I asked, "And where was it that you found it?"

"It was like this," Herr Schellendorf said, and at that point the story took an extraordinary turn.

The UB 1809-49, he told me, used to winter in the Kerguelen Islands.

I was astonished. "The Kerguelens?"

"That's right. In summer, we torpedoed ships sailing from South Africa to Australia or vice versa, and in winter we dropped anchor in the Kerguelens. There's sort of a natural harbour, Christmas Harbour, on the big island, the one where Mount Ross is. It's actually a whole bunch of islands, an archipelago, all sorts of little tiny islands, some of them no more than a rock sticking out of the sea. Whalers used to spend their winters there in the old days."

He related to me a view of the war I had never encountered, having spent the conflict somewhere else entirely, in even less hospitable surroundings. As the fighting dragged on, their submarine spent more and more time hiding, and less time looking for enemy ships to sink. The captain was a Nazi—or maybe he'd just gone along with the Nazis for the ride—but by then he had lost any enthusiasm for piracy he had ever had. As for Schellendorf, he never had any. On the Kerguelens, it never got too cold, a more or less steady ten degrees Celsius, with a constant breeze. An odd kind of wild kraut grew there, which Seliger, the ship's cook, prepared in the traditional German way for cabbage, and instead of pork he served the local wildlife: cats. There were hundreds of them on the island.

"How did they get there?"

"The whalers brought them. Cats and rats. In time, they spread to the other islands. I don't know what the rats lived on, they had to live on something, but the cats certainly lived on the rats."

He told how the bored sailors had spent their time digging in the ground, because the whalers had left behind more than just cats. They had buried or lost all kinds of artefacts, from knives with broad rusty blades, for slicing whale blubber, to broken harpoons and fishbone needles, and even a beautiful mermaid, carved out of wood and with traces of its original paint. When Torpedomeister Heinrich Hellebrandt found her, she was weathered a bleak grey, but still beautiful.

"She must have been from the prow of some whaling schooner," said Schellendorf, and added, with a lewd little chuckle, "She had breasts like two little apples. And one of her eyes was still almost blue."

Jealous of Hellebrandt's treasure, the submariners had all combed the island, practically meter by

meter, but the pickings were slim. Their best find
was a leather-bound Bible, its pages rotten with
mildew. So Schellendorf and his buddy Kurt Töppel
took to a rubber boat, going from island to island in
the hope of finding another wooden beauty. The
captain gave his permission, apparently aware that
letting the crew keep busy amusing themselves was
the best way to maintain discipline. Under cloudy
skies, on waves whipped up by the constant whistling
wind, they rocked from island to island. They found
nothing, not even a bone needle or a worn sailor's
clog. They were about to give it up, when fortune
smiled on Schellendorf.

"One islet had a slab of rock about twenty meters
square, with a bit of sand in the middle. We dug
through the sand there but found nothing. Then I
went to take a look at some seals rolling around on
the tiny beach, and saw an object poking up out of
the sand. It looked like a root, but it couldn't have
been a root, there wasn't a tree in sight.

"I ventured out among the seals. They weren't
aggressive or scared of me—there were no pups
around—and when I got to the root, I grabbed it and
gave it a yank. It slipped out of the sand and there it
was: an old bottle."

My dear Herr Enfield. Inside that bottle was the
Latin manuscript that Professor Eva Althammer and
I translated into German. Schellendorf brought it
home to Germany with him, his only souvenir of the
war. And when his friend—who could have been a
scholar had he not been expelled for some political

delict or another—told him it was in Latin and apparently valuable, he had the manuscript framed, and finally unloaded it to pay for his pipe tobacco.

Of course—as you will see—it is an obvious fraud. But how it got to the Kerguelens remains a mystery. The French scientific research station that operates there now didn't exist during the war, so it cannot be the prank of some erudite and classically educated French marine scientist. Perhaps, then, it is the prank of some erudite and classically educated whaler! There were such men among the captains of whaling ships in times past. Of course, you will surely agree (from the internal evidence) that it must have been buried in the sand on the seal island some time *after* 1837.

I am attaching a photocopy of the Latin text, and Professor Eva Althammer's German translation. If you can think of any explanation for this enigma, I would very much appreciate hearing about it from you.

Yours,
Rudolf Ceeh
Retired Engineer

P.S. I arranged to have a battery-operated wheelchair shipped to Herr Schellendorf, and when my colleague Klanger was going to visit his grandmother in the Eastern Sector in 1988, I asked him to look the old man up and bring me word of how he liked it. It turns out that after my visit, the invalid was (predictably) summoned for a friendly conversation in certain offices. There he spent three days, and was told that I was a West German spy *and* an American agent. When Klanger visited him, Schellendorf turned the story, like all his other adventures, into a barrel of laughs.

Of course, he was not allowed to have the wheelchair. It was assigned to "someone needier." And when I visited the former Eastern Sector in 1990, neither Herr Mittenberg nor the jolly old sailor was to be found on Heinrich Poltergeiststrasse, and the Ernst Erdpflügerwerke building was vacant. Which, of course, was only to be expected.

EVENTS ON THE ISLE OF TESALUS

The following is the content of Schellendorf's document, titled Events on the Isle of Tesalus, *by Questus Firmus Siculus, translated from the Latin by Clark Ashton Sprague of Arkham College, with an eye to the German translation by Dr. Eva Althammer.*

My name is Questus Firmus Siculus. My adoptive father was Gaius Firmus Siculus, and my actual father is the poet Publius Ovidius Naso, last heard of in Britain, but I am not certain whether he is still living there. After the death of Gaius Firmus, my mother, Proculeia Aemilia Saepuli, remarried to Spurius Caecina Ventro. She died in Rome in the year 782 A.U.C. Her husband took his own life shortly thereafter. The story of my life, my discoveries, and my journey across the Great Ocean are written in a book that I left in the charge of King Telalocus, in the city of Tetulapolis, in the Kingdom of the Mayus on the continent my companions and I named the New Land. The circumstances in which I am writing this report unfortunately compel brevity.

Upon the wishes of King Telalocus, we boarded the *Corinna* and sailed southward along the coast. Our destination was the mouth of the Great River, where Mayus legend places the realm of their fore-

fathers, a civilization reputedly more advanced, from
all points of view, than that of the Mayus themselves.
The passion that possessed me in Rome before I set
sail across the ocean was reawakened by the tales
King Telalocus told, and I in turn inspired my crew.
This voyage, not unlike the one we set out on from
Ostia in 784 A.U.C., was a journey into the unknown,
and it was made all the more perilous by the fact
that the constellations in these parts differ so much
from the ones over Rome and its Empire. We sailed
with only the shoreline of the New Land to guide us.
Conditions became even more difficult when an
intense heat developed, which exhausted the oarsmen.
We were obliged to rely on wind and the machine.
Fortunately, everywhere we stopped for the night, we
found sufficient fuel to keep the machine operating
while the oarsmen rested.

On our fifteenth night at sea, the sky grew cloudy,
and we were soon immersed in total darkness. We
waited in vain for dawn: the blackness persisted. The
wind kept rising and we were caught in its mighty
force far greater than any we had ever experienced in
our own seas. Poseidon, if it was he—if his powers
extend to these waters—drove us farther and farther
south, day after day. We had no means of estimating
how long we raced through the darkness, nor were
we able to be certain of our direction. All the same,
we all believed that we had been blown south,
farther south than any previous navigator.

Finally we saw daylight, but there was a dense fog
on the water, and although the wind had dropped, we

found ourselves in the power of a formidable current, still carrying us through those unknown waters in the same direction as before.

Days later the fog lifted, and we found ourselves out of sight of land. The air was much colder and the sea was full of fish. The Greek oarsmen caught them in nets or speared them, and we were able to replenish the food supplies we had almost exhausted during the interminable days we had spent helpless in the thrall of sea, wind, and darkness. With no land in sight, I gave the order to raise sails and row. The current that had carried us through the fog continued to push us onward.

The temperature kept dropping, and immense pieces of ice began to appear in the water, the kind that form in winter on rivers in the far north of the Empire. As it got colder, we pulled on breeches and wrapped ourselves in cloaks. The cold was unpleasant, but at least it made the oarsmen row ever harder in order to keep warm. We skimmed along with the current at a speed I was at a loss to estimate, passing numbers of ice cliffs in the water. Then the fog fell again and the temperature began to rise. We removed our cloaks and sailed on with the current, faster and faster. Night did not fall—it seemed like perpetual day. I am unable to say how long we sailed, there being no nights to separate the days. Nor can I name the feeling that possessed me—it was a sensation unlike any I had ever experienced, and I cannot now find the words to describe it; I fear that I will find no key in the future either. I was overcome with a

strange curiosity, a yearning to overcome the
mysteries of these terrible regions. It was evident to
me that we were rushing toward some thrilling
knowledge, a mystery that I half hoped would never
be revealed to us, for its revelation seemed so likely
to mean our doom.

When after some time the fog lifted, we found
that the ice cliffs had vanished and both air and sea
were much warmer. We sailed into the radiance of
the sun shining from low near the horizon and a
rocky island rose out of the water ahead of us.
We later found out, from the natives, that its name
was Tesalus.

On the shore we saw a group of natives, who

*This is the end of the first scroll. The text apparently was
continued on the second one, which was accidentally
destroyed by the negligent, unwitting Mr. Reimann. The
conclusion of Questus's narrative on the third scroll
follows, and I conclude with my commentary.*

having surrounded ourselves with barricades
hurriedly erected from the black wood of nearby trees.

Vitus and his barbarians have retreated, but are
lying in wait. Sooner or later we must fight our way
out of here. Out on the water, the blaze which
destroyed my ship is still smoldering. We have
built a fire in the middle of our enclosure and I am
hurrying to finish writing this report. Clearly, I cannot
hope to carry it to Rome myself. At the last possible

moment, I shall slip it into a bottle and throw it into the sea.

A native prisoner sits shackled before the fire. We were going to use him as a hostage, but I had to abandon the plan when I realized that the barbarian king places no value on his people, and a hostage would serve no purpose. I turn to look at him, and he grins at me, his thick lips of the sort that some Moors have, and he pulls down his lower lip with his index finger. His teeth are all black, but apparently healthy, since they gleam like polished ebony. He stares at me with black eyes that I cannot fathom. His eyes have no whites, they are all black, as is his skin, the palms of his hands, his fingernails, everything. I flinch from his gaze (which feels like all Hades staring at me) and quickly return to my writing.

When I have completed this report and sealed it in a bottle, I shall give the order to attack.

Most of the oarsmen have put on their armor and taken up the shields and short swords of legionaries.

The barbarians are all around us, crouching behind the black rocks and bushes, but with our swords we will be able to hack our way through them to the boat that is hidden in the bay. Once we are on our way I shall entrust this report to the ocean waves. Then our destiny will be in the hands of Poseidon, and surely Jove will protect us as he has throughout our voyage in these strange ends of the earth. Or perhaps it will be Aristotle's god who will help us, that is, if he takes any interest at all in the fate of human beings.

I think of my beloved mother, Proculeia, and my father, Ovid.

I shall now give the order to attack.

Questus Firmus Siculus

CCCMLXXXIV [A.U.C]

COMMENTARY

Mr. Ceeh's remark that the bottle with the manuscript must of necessity have been concealed on Seal Island after 1837 was not mysterious to me; I am, after all, an American literary man. That was the year that Edgar Allan Poe published his only novel, *The Narrative of Arthur Gordon Pym of Nantucket*. It was also clear to me (if not to Mr. Ceeh) why the erudite Dr. Althammer declared the letter from the bottle a fraud immediately upon reading it. I am not much of an optimist, but I do believe that most American graduates will not need any explanation either. There will be many foreign readers of Questus's story, however, so perhaps some basic facts about Poe's classic book are in order. (As for graduates of universities outside America, I am not so pessimistic.)

The work is an adventure novel about a journey to unknown southern seas. In Poe's day, such books were very popular. Authors sometimes made them out to be authentic records of actual events, and sometimes they actually were.

The novel's hero, A. G. Pym (note the similarity to the name of E. A. Poe), experiences multifarious frightening and grisly adventures on the deck of the brig *Grampus*, and after a wild storm ultimately causes the ship to capsize, he and some companions survive on its overturned bottom. There he even stoops to cannibalism. A number of days later, when only Pym and one sailor, Dirk Peters, are left alive, they are picked up by the schooner *Jane Guy*, sailing southward to hunt seals and other creatures of the sea that are in demand on the American market.

The ship sails further south than any before them ever has, and, at latitude 83° 20' south and longitude 43° 5' west—that is, on the Antarctic continent, the existence of which would have been completely unknown to Poe—they come upon an island that they later learn is called Tsalal. The prevailing color on the island is black—bushes, rocks, birds are all black, and of course, so are its native inhabitants. They have no whites to their black eyes, and when, later on, one of them pulls his thick lips apart with his fingers, the surprised Pym discovers that even his teeth are black.

For some time, the natives and their chief Too-wit are friendly, but in the end they ambush the *Jane Guy* crew in a narrow ravine. Once again, only Pym and Peters escape death. The natives also succeed in setting the *Jane Guy* on fire, resulting in its cargo of gunpowder exploding, which frightens the natives into absquatulating. In the end, Pym and Peters succeed in commandeering one of the natives' canoes and, pursued by the natives, row it out onto the high sea, where an eerie ocean current seizes them and carries them southward. Instead of getting colder, it gets warmer and warmer; a fog falls on the sea, with huge white birds flying in it, and suddenly the adventurers come upon a chasm in the ocean, with an immense white figure rising out of it.

It is here that Pym's narrative ends. And so might the "Questus" narrative that so closely follows Poe. But in the editor's note that follows Pym's tale, we are told that Pym and Peters escaped somehow and found their way back to the United States. There, at the request of the editor, E. A. Poe, Pym wrote down his story, but unfortunately died before he could complete the work.

Of course, Poe was using authorial license: both Pym and his narrative are fiction—the fantastic progeny of Poe's imagination.

I trust that this *précis* will explain to the reader why Dr. Althammer was so certain, upon one reading, that the manuscript is a fraud. On Tesalus, the island described by Questus, the colour black also prevails, his "Moor" also has black teeth and his eyes lack whites. Further, the temperature increases as they travel southward instead of dropping to arctic cold. Questus makes a habit of Latinizing names, not always precisely, so it is not hard to extrapolate Poe's Tsalal from the Tesalus of Questus, and to see that the name of the native chief Vitus could have come about by reversing the syllables of Poe's Too-wit, with Questus appending the customary Latin suffix.

The new "Questus" manuscript, like the earlier one found by the archaeology students, was entrusted to two independent teams of experts—one scroll to each of two different universities—who conducted all the same chemical and linguistic tests. Startlingly, the results were unanimous: this, too, is an authentic manuscript of the first century A.D.

So, was there an island called Tsalal, perhaps in some bay on the coast of Antarctica?

If the second Questus text is no more a falsification than the first one—and I have no choice but to believe the experts that it is not—then either Poe was gifted with some kind of supernatural imagination, or else he found his way to some arcane sources, perhaps the logs or memoirs of ship's captains from the early nineteenth century. Of course, that is extremely improbable.

I am convinced that we must dismiss the idea that the Questus manuscript could be as much a fiction as Pym's. Too much scholarly expertise confirms that Questus was describing actual events and circumstances.

Summa summarum, then: Questus did not solve for us the mystery of Ovid's banishment. In addition, he bequeathed to us more mysteries, and these far more inexplicable; I doubt they will ever be explained.

P. O. E.

LETTER FROM MLLE MURIEL BLAIVE

To this, the fourth, edition of the Questus narrative, I append the letter received after the publication of the French translation of the third edition.

Dear Mr. Enfield,

I am a student of French literature, and am working on my doctoral dissertation on the topic of the influence of American literature on the work of Jules Verne. While working in the archives of the National Library in Paris, I chanced upon something singular, which will undoubtedly be of interest to you.

Within the context of my doctoral work, the most significant of Verne's books with a link to the United States in general, and to American literature in particular, is his 1897 novel *Le sphinx des glaces* (translated into English as *The Sphinx of the Ice-Fields*). It is Verne's completion of Poe's novel *The Narrative of Arthur Gordon Pym*, in which Verne provides realistic, scientific explanations—one of his specialities—for all the inexplicable mysteries in Poe's text.

The novel begins in the Kerguelen Islands (odd, is it not, *cher monsieur*, considering the letter of Mr. Ceeh?) where its hero, an American naturalist studying Antarctic regions, boards the brig *Halbrane*, under a Captain Len Guy. It turns out that he is the brother of Captain William Guy of the ship *Jane Guy*. The captain of the *Halbrane* does not believe that his brother actually perished, and is launching an expedition to discover what happened to him. The American joins the expedition, and later in the journey Pym's old companion, Dirk Peters, joins them on the ship. He too is convinced that his idol, Pym, is still alive. After many adventures, including a shipwreck, the adventurers approach the Antarctic, where surprising events overtake them.

Verne's original manuscript of *Le sphinx des glaces* has been preserved in the archives of his publisher, J. Hetzel & Cie., complete with marginal annotations. Some are in black ink, and from their context in the manuscript appear to be those of the author. By far the majority of the marginal notes, however, are in red ink, clearly in another handwriting, and appear to be those of the book's editor.

Toward the end of the book Verne's castaways confront a "sphinx of ice," an immense ice cliff on the Antarctic coast, and on its wall they find the frozen corpse of Arthur Gordon Pym! You will recall that Poe's story ends with Pym's canoe being drawn to the south by some mysterious force. In Verne's novel, as soon as the *Paracuta*, a boat bearing the castaways, approaches the "sphinx of ice," every metallic object on board (knives, pots, firearms, etc.) flies up into the air and hurtles towards the cliff. It turns out to be a massive magnet, perhaps the earth's magnetic south pole. The *Paracuta* lands beside it and on one face of the "sphinx" they find all the metal objects ripped away from them by the magnet. They walk around "the monster's right paw," and there they find Pym's body. His ship had also come within the force field of the magnet, and the unfortunate man had had a musket slung over his shoulder. The magnetic force of the sphinx had seized the weapon, and with it Arthur Gordon Pym, pinning him to the cliff by the gun strapped across his chest.

Verne describes Pym's corpse as being almost naked, preserved intact by the cold, with a white beard down to his waist and the nails on his hands and feet so long they resembled claws—evidence that, unable to extricate himself from the strap holding the fateful gun, Pym had lived for some time on the wall of the sphinx.

At this point in the manuscript, there is in the margin the proofreader's symbol for "delete" in red ink, and several lines in the text are struck out with the same ink. They are still clearly legible, and they read:

Beside Pym's corpse hung the remains of another man, his mummified body encased in something resembling the strip armour of ancient Roman legionaries (*lorica segmentata*), still recognizable though almost eaten away with rust. At the foot of the cliff beneath this second corpse—obviously much older than Pym's—lay the vestiges of the typical Roman legionary's shield. On its rim was an inscription, apparently, in the Roman fashion, the name of its owner. Only a few letters of the inscription were legible: Q ... MVS SIC ....

In the novel of an author who prided himself on adhering meticulously to the possible (or at least what was perceived as possible in the late nineteenth century), the editor apparently viewed this fantastic bit as being a departure from Verne's principles and so he deleted the mention of the Roman legionary.

In the light of the document submitted to you, *cher monsieur*, by Mr. Ceeh and of your hypotheses, the unfortunate dead man hanging beside Pym is well within the realm of "the possible." What remains unexplained is how he found his way into Verne's text.

Sincerely yours,

Muriel Blaive, M.A.

COMMENTARY

F rench scholars and scientists have examined Verne's manuscript, and most particularly the section where the editor had deleted the passage about Questus, and have authenticated it "beyond the shadow of a doubt," in the words of the American juridical cliché.

What can I add to the letter of the charming Mlle Blaive? Nothing, except perhaps to paraphrase Hamlet, that there are confoundedly many things between heaven and earth.

PATRICK OLIVER ENFIELD
Redington Shores, Florida
January–April 1998
DEO GRATIAS!

AUTHOR'S NOTE

JOSEF SKVORECKY

Like a lot of old people who don't fall asleep as easily as they used to, for years I've used a technique for helping myself go to sleep. Instead of counting sheep going across a bridge, I think up stories. For a long time it was a tale called "The Beautiful Girl from the Kerguelen Islands," in which the hero travels in a small plane chartered in India, feeding albatrosses in the air en route. The Kerguelens have held a certain magic for me ever since I was a lad and read Poe's *Narrative of Arthur Gordon Pym of Nantucket* and Verne's sequel to that fantastic book, *The Sphinx of the Ice-Fields*. For several years of our exile from our homeland, my late friend Karel F. V. Salaquarda and I contemplated making the journey to the Kerguelens, for me to write about them for *National Geographic* and for him to take the pictures.

But we ran into problems. The Kerguelen Islands belong to France. They were discovered in 1772 by the Breton Captain Yves de Kerguelen-Trémarec, who first convinced King Louis XV that it was a region with diamonds to be mined, along with rubies, marble, coal, and trees to be felled in dense forests.

The fact is that, unable to land there, he had only seen the islands through a thick fog, so he employed the imagination of an explorer. This whetted the King's appetite, and he sent Captain de Kerguelen back to the commercially promising archipelago. This time some of the crew succeeded in making it to shore and they saw what they saw. Upon his return, Kerguelen had to own up to His Majesty: the islands, he said, "are more inhospitable than Iceland, uninhabited and uninhabitable." Louis XV had him locked up for it, but not in the Bastille, only in a posh jail in a castle in the Loire Valley. In so doing, he saved the man's life: when the Revolution broke out, the King went to the guillotine, but Kerguelen was named chief intendant of the Port of Brest because, despite being an aristocrat, he was considered one of the tyrant's victims. The lucky unfortunate lived out the rest of his life in peace there. He died in 1797.

At the time Salaquarda and I were doing the research, there was no normal transportation to the Kerguelens by ship or by plane. (I wonder if that's not the case to this day.) A French meteorological station was situated there, and once every two or three months a French warship would stop by to drop off food and medicine. Somehow, one Soviet meteorologist found his way there. As a scientist, he was officially a guest of the French government. He took a good look around and asked for political asylum on the Kerguelen Islands. Whether he was as fortunate as the imaginative Kerguelen, I have no idea.

We discovered some other interesting things. During the Second World War, the German Kriegsmarine had a naval base on the islands. From there, they used to waylay Allied merchant ships sailing in the south seas between America, Africa, and India. All this sparked our interest even more, but then I got asthma, Karel Salaquarda's health began to fail, and after some time he died prematurely. So much for our romantic dream.

Nevertheless, I kept on dreaming about the beautiful girl from the Kerguelen Islands and the tame albatross. Along with this romance, however, following the example of Walter Mitty, I wove many other stories on the edge of sleep. One that kept coming back was the tale of Rome.

When I graduated from high school and Latin was no longer compulsory for me, I developed an interest in things I neglected in school. Somewhere I had read a hypothesis that, had the Roman Empire not fallen, and had it not been for the subsequent centuries of a religious orthodoxy hostile to science, the Romans—whose technology was quite advanced during the final centuries of the Empire—might have developed the first steam engine as early as A.D. 1000, and the first aircraft perhaps a century later. Back then I started weaving a story about a disappointed Roman senator whose son refuses to take up the military career expected for such youths, but instead invents little carts that move by themselves, which his father considers kiddy toys. The shrewd Augustus Caesar, however, is quick to recognize how valuable such carts could be to the military as assault vehicles, and in the end, they are.

For a long time, that was just a story that rested in the fog between my waking and my sleeping. Then, in the winter of 1998, in Redington Shores, Florida, on my daily morning stroll along the shore of the Gulf of Mexico, it occurred to me to take all those silly bits—Pym, *The Sphinx of the Ice-Fields*, the dream of the Kerguelens, the dream of the Roman inventor of steam engines, and a magical expedition from Lovecraft's Miskatonic University—and combine them with the tragedy of Publius Ovidius Naso. That is, Ovid, exiled by Augustus Caesar to Tomis on the Black Sea (modern Costanza, in Romania), where he would have strolled along the beach like me, until in the end he died there and the world never found out what it was that he had done to the Emperor to get himself exiled.

Over the centuries, there have been numerous attempts to explain that enigma, but none that was particularly convincing. It occurred to me that part of my story could be a play, say, a farce, written by Ovid in his exile, containing the explanation of his tragic disagreement with Augustus.

Of course, I'm no playwright, but I was visited by an inspiration: what if the manuscript of the farce were preserved only in the form of incoherent fragments? In the final analysis, Ovid would have written it in the first century A.D., so logically, the manuscript would have undergone considerable deterioration, and I could justifiably contend that Ovid had explained the whole affair in his play and not explain anything at all myself.

This mystification gave birth to the expedition from Miskatonic University to the Mayan Copán and the discovery of Ovid's manuscript; this, in turn, brought into the world Questus, the young inventor, love child of Ovid and the beautiful Proculeia, whose destiny is entwined with those of Shakespeare's King Cymbeline, the German sailor Schellendorf, Feydeau aficionado Monsieur Fouillet, Miss Muriel Blaive, and the rest.

In the process, I was constantly aware of the presence of Edgar Allen Poe. He made his way into the story through many chinks, not the least of which were the initials of Patrick Oliver Enfield, the writer of mysteries who edited the Questus manuscript for the modern reader, and several quotations from his works which Mr. Enfield, apparently not well versed in American literature, failed to recognize.

With God's help I assembled it all and set it down on paper in the Year of Our Lord 1998 on the shores of the magical Gulf of Mexico.

J.S.

Sources

Aries, Philippe, and George Duby, general editors.
*A History of Private Life, Volume 1: From Pagan
Rome to Byzantium*. Paul Veyne, editor. Translated
by Arthur Goldhammer (originally published as
Historie de la Vie Privée, Editions du Seuil, 1985).
Cambridge, Mass.: Belknap Press of Harvard
University Press, 1992.

Boardman, John, Jasper Griffin and Oswyn Murray,
general editors. *The Oxford History of the Classical
World, Volume 2: The Roman World*.
Oxford: Oxford University Press, 1986.

Bunson, Matthew. *Encyclopedia of the Roman Empire*.
New York: Facts on File, Inc., 1994.

Carcopino, Jerome. *Daily Life in Ancient Rome*.
1941. Trans. E. O. Lorimer.
London: Penguin Books, 1991.

Jones, Peter and Keith Sidwell. *The World of Rome:
An Introduction to Roman Culture*.
Cambridge: Cambridge University Press, 1997.

Ovid. *The Poems of Exile*. Translated, with
introduction, notes and glossary, by Peter Green.
London: Penguin Books, 1994.

———. *The Erotic Poems*. Translated by Peter Green.
London: Penguin Books, 1982.

Parker, Geoffrey, editor. *The Cambridge Illustrated
History of Warfare*. Cambridge: Cambridge University
Press, 1995.